Percival H. W Almy

Scintillæ carmenis

Percival H. W Almy

Scintillæ carmenis

ISBN/EAN: 9783743309210

Manufactured in Europe, USA, Canada, Australia, Japa

Cover: Foto ©Andreas Hilbeck / pixelio.de

Manufactured and distributed by brebook publishing software
(www.brebook.com)

Percival H. W Almy

Scintillæ carmenis

BY

PERCIVAL H. W. ALMY.

LONDON:
ELLIOT STOCK, 62, PATERNOSTER ROW, E.C.
1895.

CONTENTS

Contents

PELEUS AND THETIS.

PART I.

THE blue Ægean wrapt about her isles,
The beautiful Ægean ! . . .
       *   *   *   *   *
Who sits upon the lone Thermean shore,
What time the sun goes down between the hills
Of Ossa and Olympus ?   What fair form
Sits on the jutted rock, and with a hand
Of more than Chian whiteness arched above
The sorrow of her eyes, sweeps the dark waves,
As one who looks the coming of her love ?
Who sits upon the lone Thermean shore ?
Is it a nymph—a god ?   A wandering wind,
Borne down along the laurels, has tossed back
The burden of her hair, and left her breast
Naked beneath the modest gaze of night ;
Her lips are riven with a sob ; her eyes
Gloomy and sunken as a woodland well,
When the last star that saw its brightness there
Has died beneath a cloud.
Who sits upon the lone Thermean shore,
Upon a broken rock beneath the vines ?
Thetis ! Thetis !   Her snowy hand slips down,

I

Down to the dimpled apple of her chin :
It is—it is the maid of Thessaly !
And the blue sea is kneeling at her feet,
And the soft wind is listening to her sighs :
'And what though he be young, and brave, and fair,
Must I who might have clasped the neck of Jove,
Must I whose lips have felt the kiss of him
Who grasps the empire of the isles, must I
Whom all the gods call fairest of the fair,
Stoop to the toying of a mortal hand,
And sell my birthright immortality
For a brief age of love ?   How could I bear,
Alone among the ocean's icy halls,
The coldness of the nymphs ?   How could I bear
The haughty toss of Amatheia's head,
The laugh of Amphithoe, the blank gaze,
Half scorn, half wonder, of Alia's eye,
Nesea's chill advice—the whispered doubt
Of slow Dexamine ?   No ! no ! I daren't.
Can this be she, the whisperers would say,
Who late, upon the car of shells, sate next
The father of the isles, and with white hand
Toying the yielded trident, cast a look
Of deigning pity on the sister nymphs
Who sported in the wake-ward foam, as though,
Less favoured, they were aught less fair than she !
Pride builds her shrine at Paphos, and demands
Of human hearts a daily sacrifice.'

She ceased—a sound as of a splashing oar
Followed the lute-like plainings of her voice,
And round the rocks that fold the bay to rest,
Shot a light shallop, built of cypress wood,
Sewn with a lion's hide against the sea,

And bearing one lone form upon the thwarts.
With eager eyes and beating heart, she watched
The progress of the boat among the shades ;
'Neath shelving coasts hung wild with tangled vines
Down sloping to the sea, by creeks and grots
Full of the sounds of fountains, it did move,
Till high upon the shallow beach it paused.
She knew it was the barque of Peleus,
And when the lonely occupant leapt forth,
And moved with rapid strides along the shore,
Like one who lingers o'er a forced farewell,
So lingered she beside her native wave,
Loath to depart, yet fearing to remain.

Meantime the being of the boat drew near ;
A lynx-hide drooped about his loins succinct,
Suspended by a golden studded zone ;
And clashing at his thigh, a silver horn
Gleamed in the flood light of the rising moon
Like a wreathed flame ; a triple-stranded net,
Knotted and noosed of fine Phasisan flax,
Hung at his belt ; and in his hand he grasped
A mighty hunting spear—full five palms long,
With guards of steel and haft of corneil wood,
The gift of Chiron, father of the hunt.

'O ! harder than the flints of Marpessa'—
So cried he on the rocks far off—
'O ! harder than the flints of Marpessa,
Is love not worthy the return of love ?
The stream reflects its stooping margin flowers,
The hills sing response to the bittern's cry,
The leaves dance to the piping of the gale—
All beauty is the print of Beauty's foot,

And Nature but an echo of herself.
And is love echoless ? are maiden hearts
Exempt from this so universal law ?
Alas ! I fear me I have loved too well ;
When passion hits the mid-noon arc of heaven,
The heart that sits beneath is shadowless.'

'Cupid has wings,' the maiden voice returned—
' Who loves indeed, who follows long and hard,
Shall win at last the apple and the rose.'

So said the maid, and kissing her wet hand,
Plunged deep into the sea.   Swift as a thought,
Flinging his shining implements aside,
He followed her.   The trembling foam arose
And mantled up her limbs as with a robe ;
The land went down, the waves grew deep and cold,
Still, hugging at the bare breast of the sea,
Or diving 'neath the surface like a mew,
The naiad fled, the Argive followed her.
Now she is just beneath his grasp—and now,
Shaking her dripping tresses far away,
She wantons wave-like with the waves, and makes
The waters dance with laughter unconfined.
Then leaping half out of the naked sea,
Turning, she looked upon the weary chase,
And offering her arms to his embrace,
Seemed waiting for the capture—will she yield ?
His heart beats high—he nears the shining goal,
He stretches forth his hand to grasp the prize,
When lo ! swift from the ridges of the sea,
A white-winged alcyon rose ; with hovering cry,
Three times it wheeled about the swimmer's head,
Then plunged into the shadows of the east,

And all the heavens were still beneath the stars :
The lover was alone upon the sea.

PART II.

A little island sitteth in the sea,
Facing the moon-born torrent of the Nile.
Among the bays that hang their golden loops,
In deep festoons, about the foam-belt coasts,
One there is fairer far than all the rest.
'Tis a mere chasm in between the rocks ;
The waves have bit the seaboard hills in two,
And, harried by the moon, at times do ride
Unchecked into the pine woods in the rear.
Yea—'tis a shepherd's tale—upon a time
They moved right up into the island's heart,
And swept away the flocks that used to feed,
Foam-white, among the dells and meadows there.
But be this so or not, 'tis a sweet spot,
And when the noon rests on her golden wheel
A little breathing space above the pines,
And the swift waves, with knees unstrung with heat,
Lie faint and motionless along the shore,
Here wont old Prœtus and his herds to rest
Until the fire of day was somewhat spent.
Now twenty suns had gone into the west
Since Thetis' love-chase o'er the moon-foiled sea.
It was the noon, the aged sea-god slept,
When, through the harbour's stony portal way,
A hide-bound skippet came : it was the same
That broke the shadow-musings of the nymph
That night beside the sea at Thessaly.
The dauntless lover stood upon the prow,
And as the vessel staggered to the shore,

Leaping upon thwarts, ' Seer of the sea,
Seer of the sea, attend,' the hero cried.
'Three times, with lifted hands and suppliant voice,
Standing upon the rocks of Thessaly,
I sued with love a daughter of the sea :
Three times with alcyon's wing or dolphin's fin,
On foot thrice swifter than a Libyan pard,
She fled the plea of open heart and arms,
And left me sorrowing beside the sea,
And left me sorrowing, but still resolved.
Seer of the sea, attend !
How may the maid of Thessaly be won ?
If I have watched the coming of her steps,
Oblivious to the call of forest horn ;
If I have dwelt whole days beside the sea,
If haply riding on the white-necked waves,
Or stretched at rest beneath the caverned rocks,
This sister of my spirit might be seen ;
If thrice with lifted hands and suppliant voice,
Standing afar, I have besought her with
The ceaseless importunity of love ;
If I have brought the purest plumaged doves,
The lushest honey and the freshest fruit,
And, on the rocks at evening, offered them
A token of—a sacrifice to love ;
If I have prayed and prayed as never priest,
And vowed and vowed as never penitent—
And *all* of no avail—say, ocean sage,
How may the maid be won ?—Devise ! devise !
If love is echoless, what plot or plan
Of force or fraud will compass my desire—
Say, ocean sage, how Thetis may be won.'
The sea-god heard, and, raising his hoar head,
Beheld the dauntless suppliant—beheld

And would by swift Protean change have fled;
But, like the breath of spring among the vines,
The name of Thetis stirred the old man's heart
To something of the greenness of its youth,
And held him though it were against his will.
Time was when but the mention of that name
Had made him face the boar of Calydon,
Or rob the Thracian lion of his hide,
But ah! his lips knew not ambrosia,
And he was old, while she was young for ever.
Something there was of sadness in his voice,
When, lifting up his head, the old man spake:
'In Thessaly, blue-veined with lucid brooks,
Within the murmur of the stream that comes
With half-drowned flowers upon its breast from Tempe,
Beside the western sea, there is a cave;
The wanderer that way can scarcely fail
To mark how goldenly the sand doth gleam,
How bright the flowers, how various the shells,
The sea hath left near this particular spot,
For 'tis the home of Thetis, and the sea,
In its impetuous adoration, loves
To bring the richest treasures of his realm
And heap them at the threshold: thither haste,
And when the moon is on the sea, and she,
Unconscious of the danger, nestles warm,
Wrapped round with maiden dream-wings, steal on her;
Let naught deter, let naught dissuade—be bold!—
With heart resolved approach the sleeping maid,
Then fling thy arms about her and hold fast,
Till, worn with useless struggles, at thy feet
She yields herself the captive of thy love;
This done, the maiden of the sea is thine.
Let not her struggles weaken thy resolve:

High ends are only gained by daring deeds ;
Be bold ! be bold !—again I say, be bold !'
So ended he, and with a look, part scorn
And part indifference, regardless of
Protested thanks and vows of sacrifice,
Declined his head and slept among the herds.
Then with a deep dip of the ocean sweeps,
A loose unfurling of the panther hide,
The vessel started like an unleashed hound
And foamed amid the sea ; free flowed the wind,
And soon a reeling blot amid the blue,
And in the wake a broadening arrow-head ;
And soon a bead wedged in 'twixt sky and sea
And flatness in the bay ;
And soon a clear horizon on all sides,
The heavy breath of slumber on the shore,
The silence of the sunset and the sea.

Part III.

'Twas night beside the sea at Thessaly.
Lo ! toss'd at anchor in the harbour's mouth,
The boat of Peleus ; and on the shore,
Where a break in the cliffs let in the moon,
With cautious tread, slow merging into view,
Th' enamoured errant of the sea himself.
With hushing finger pressed against his lips,
Tiptoe beneath the rocks, the wanderer went,
Till, at the entrance of a cave, he paused.
A sound as of the breath of one who slept
Stole from within ; the destinies were kind.
He passed the threshold overhung with vines
Laden with purple fruit beneath the moon,
And stood within the sea-god's palace hall.

A pile of cedar gathered from the sea
Burnt low upon a marble hearth ;
The walls and roof were deep inlaid with shells
Of every shape and hue beneath the sea ;
From the large fountain shell that rolls unseen
Beneath the waters of the Parthian main,
Down to the tiny harp, blood-stained, that strews
The sloping coasts of western Libya :
Cowries and pearls, sea-ears and Triton's horns,
Yea, all of strange or fair from every clime,
Or lipped, or hinged, or fluted, or convolved,
That, glistening in the cedar's scented flame,
Made up a scene fantastically fair.
A cup of gold, the wine-god's gift, high wrought
With subtlest cunning in the Lemnian forge,
Stood full of honey in a niche of pearl,
The offering haply of some pious swain,
At evening, of the shores of Phthiotis :
And leaning on a basalt shaft, hard by
The cavern's entrance, a seven-chorded lyre,
Formed from a hollow turtle-shell, and strung
With the lithe tendons of a young sea-horse.
All this he saw as in a dream ; and there,
Upon a bed of purple moss, her limbs
Swathed only in the folds of her dark hair,
Reclined the sleeping goddess of the sea.
He neared the sleeping form ; one step misplaced,
One breath too loud, and leaping from her dreams,
On Protean wings the maiden-god had fled ;
He blessed the waves that murmuring at the door
Subdued all other sounds, and with a prayer
That she who watches the events of love
Would send a happy issue, he drew near.
A while he bent over her ; still she slept :

She seemed enveloped in a sort of haze :
Her cheek was·pillowed in her arm, her chin
Nestled between her breasts, her limbs curled up,
One hand just clasped between her knees—enough !
He could endure no more ; with maddened blood,
With eyes half blind with beauty, and a sense
Of something grasping at his heart and brain,
Stooping, he touched the sleeping lips and wound
The goddess in his arms.   With breathless cry
She struggled to her feet and would have fled ;
She knew her captor, felt his grasp, and mad,
With lifted knee pressed hard against his chest,
With fingers at his throat, her limbs twined in
And locked with his, she struggled to be free.
Long time the strife continued, till at last,
Worn with contention, but unbroken still,
Glaring large-eyed defiance at her foe,
'And who art thou,' she gasped, 'who, thus profane,
Steal'st on a goddess' slumbers with intent ?—
Heaven knows with what intent.'
'The victim of your beauty,' he replied,
'And you, fair maid, the captive of my strength.'
'Never !' she shrieked ; 'O, am I not divine !'
As if the thought inspired her with a strength
Untried before, she started from his grasp,
And in another moment had been gone ;
But he with hand stretched out had caught the flow
Of her loose hair and held her captive still ;
More fierce the struggle that ensued than aught
The silence had been witness to before :
With starting eyes, with veins like knotted steel,
With teeth firm set, and breath that came and went
In quick interspirations, to and fro,
Locked in his arms the struggling maiden reeled.

But he, with every effort, nearer drew
The captive to himself.   O, will she yield?
'Tis the last struggle between love and pride!
She fights against her heart!   She fights no more!
Sinking upon her knees, with broken voice,
' I yield,' she sobbed, ' but only yield to love !'
' Then be henceforth the captive of my heart ;
My arms compel no more.'   His hold relaxed ;
She did not now attempt to fly from him ;
She did not speak, she did not even move,
But only clung about his knees and wept.
He raised her up ; she fell upon his neck
With passionate sobs.   ' O, love me well !' she cried ;
' I've given up all for love.'   He pressed her lips—
She asked no more—it was reply enough,
And with a smile that made the tears more fair,
Raising her head, she kissed him in return ;
No need of other vows ; their love was told ;
Their troth was plight; henceforth their lives were one.

    *   *   *   *   *

They sat within the entrance of the cave,   ·
Upon the fragment of a rock.   How calm,
How still, the night!   Just opposite the spot,
Divided by a narrow slip of sea,
There was a little isle ; above the pines
Towered up the ruined turrets of a fane,
Once sacred to Diana, and, near by,
A moonlit gap among the trees revealed
A statue of the god : her nervous limbs
Were weather-stained and overgrown with moss,
Her bow, the symbol of her office, broke,
And tangled weeds sprung high above her knees.
There, to the left, deep sunken like a bowl,
And bordered with the shadows of the hills,

There was a meadow, dotted o'er with sheep,
A fountain in the centre ; even here
The chuckle of the waters might be heard.
An altar built with rustic skill stood by,
Yet smoking with the evening sacrifice
Of some home-faring swain ; and far beyond
There was the blue Ægean, calm and still,
Its surface scolloped with the least of winds,
And one lone fisher-sail, just visible,
Foam-white upon the far horizon line.
All this the lovers saw, yet neither spake ;
To human hearts, however placed, there comes
A sort of sadness when the race is won ;
The inspiration of pursuit has gone ;
Ambition suddenly grows objectless ;
And we would almost tread the course again,
If only to fill up the blank produced
By pleasure merely passive and assured.
Darkly this feeling came to him to-night,
And, fostered by the stillness, grew at last
Into a sense almost of pain ; while she,
Awed by the seeming sternness of his look,
Gazed earnestly upon him, but spoke not.
At length, aroused as from a dream, he turned
And looked into her upturned eyes and smiled.
Then one strong arm stole warmly round her waist,
And drawing her more closely to his side,
He pressed one lingering kiss upon her lips :
' Mine ! mine !' he murmured, and she whispered back,
' Yes ! yes, love ! ever thine.'

Part IV.

Now was the marriage-day ; from dawn till noon,
Up the steep sides of Pelion, was heard
The clash of axletrees, the neigh of steeds,
The muffled tumult of a thousand feet,
Slow moving to the din of beaten drums.
A troop of virgins with disordered stoles
And hair flower-trammelled, led along the van,
And waving dew-wet rose boughs, chanted songs
In honour of the bridegroom and the bride.
A band of shepherd youths moved close behind,
With jars of wine, and baskets heaped with fruit,
And milk, and wheat, and honey for the gods.
Next came a crowd confused of youths and maids,
With laugh and dance and clamorous ' Evoe !'
Aping the mode of Silenus and Pan :
And girls with Phœbean crescents on their brows,
And new-crowned Venuses with careless hair,
And Bacchants hardly managing the pards.
Then came the loose-robed priests with crowns of
        leaves,
And brazen chariots, and milk-white steeds,
And groups of slaves with burdens on their heads,
And dogs, and mules, and children with bare limbs,
And aged sires, who told with kindling eyes
Of fierce encounters with the moon-sent boar ;
And matrons who on every wedding-day
Live o'er again their own.
Others apart kept up the game of love :
Here, set in order, two contending bands
Waged war with flowers and apples ; there a youth
Held back a struggling beauty by the curls,
And stopped her cries with kisses in the mouth.

And so the mighty cavalcade moved on,
Such cries, such shouts, such laughter, such a hum
Of music in the hollows of the hills !
The soaring eagle caught the sound, and paused
Just on the threshold of the mint of day;
The heaven-bound lark stood still; the mountain goat
Crept from its shy retreat among the vines,
And stood with hoofs streaming with trodden wine,
Mute gazing on a scene so wild and fair.

But now the halls of Chiron were in sight :
Column and obelisk and dome of gold,
Burning beneath the noon, the fabric stood.
The nearer view disclosed, as though a mist
Of golden exhalations, scenes at once
More fair, more vast, and more magnificent ;
Arches and porticos and deep arcades,
On shafts of jasper, capitalled with gold,
Upheld athwart a diamond-lighted gloom,
Inter-irradiated by the flash,
The gleam, of many-gemmed intaglios ;
Turrets and terraces aglow with hues
Of amethyst and pearl; and lofty spires,
And far-extending galleries, whose fronts,
Nervous with sapphire light, seemed but the dream,
The mist of what they were ; deep-darkening aisles,
Far-winding colonnades, and avenues
Of pillars labyrinthinely involved ;
Such and so glorious were the scenes disclosed,
Sudden between two woods of shadowy pine,
Upon the eagle peak of Pelion.

At noon the gods came down ; a mist of gold
Hung over all the hill; the sound of wings ;

The break of wheels ; the muffled hum of harps ;
A rush, a flash, a beam amid the mist,
Down came the doves of Paphos, down the car,
' Venus !' the people shouted : ' Venus Queen !'
She stood aloft, she shook the streaming reins ;
Her tunic, slipping from her shoulder, bared
One blue-veined pillow to the blush of day ;
Her limbs distilled the breath of frankincense ;   .
Her feet gleamed pink beneath the twisted strings
That held them in the sandals ; and her hair,
Slipping the silver cincture, fell in folds
About her throat and neck. ' Venus !' they cried,
' Venus !' the people cried : ' Evoe ! Evoe !'
And ere the sound had died among the dells,
Down the highway of thunder-folded clouds,
With braze of trumpets and the swing of wings,
The car of Carthage came. . . .
High in the midst reclined the wife of Jove ;
Her camus, purple purfled, spilt with pearls,
Laced with a braid of gold between the breasts,
Revealed the queenly fulness of her port ;
Her eyes saw not the crowd ; a loveless smile,
Like moonlight mirror'd in a rift of ice,
Played round her lips : no tongue could speak for awe,
No eye behold.   But lo ! the other gods :
Then came the belted mistress of the wise ;
And Ceres sun-burnt from between the sheaves ;
And Bacchus with the tipsy poppy crown,
And purple feet from trampled winepresses ;
And Dian with her bare legs torn with thorns ;
And Neptune with his cloak of foam-fringed blue,
Clasped with a tropic pearl beneath the throat ;
And Phœbus with his harp upon his back,
Locks, laurels, dripping with anointing oil,

And all the Muses following in the rear,
With Delphic snatches of an old, old song.
Last came the father of the gods himself:
There was a sound of thunder in the hills,
A stagnance in the air; a stifling cloud,
Such as precedes the coming of the storm,
Involved the mountain in a haze of brass;
Earth shook with all its weight of streams and hills;
Then, as all eyes were fixed upon the heavens,
And every heart grew still,
Above the tallest of the forest pines
Gleamed out the car of thunder; in the midst,
Like some high marble column, stood the god;
His robe had slipped the gird and streamed behind
In volumes to the gale; instinct he turned
To catch the heavy folds from off the wind,
And all the tensioned prowess of his limbs
At once made visible.   The God! the God!
The flaming car alighted in the midst;
The crowd fell back, the god moved to their head,
And the Olympian palace halls were empty.
High up the palace steps, on either hand
Gazed at by volunt lions, they did pass;
Beneath the porch of pillars, down the aisle
Into the banquet-chamber at the end.
Here scenes of splendour unsurpassed by aught
That Fancy ever feigned accosted them:
The deep-domed roof, gold-chased; the marble floor;
The walls of alabaster, tapestried
(Idalian love-scenes wrought in silk and gold,
By Argive maidens, at the close of day,
Upon the lonely threshold of the sea);
The pillars dashed with essences and wreathed
With heavy folded Tyrian; the doors

With golden panels, golden-hinged, that swung
Soundlessly into cold-slabbed baths; the courts,
Shadowy and vast, twixt Parian pillars seen,
With intervening glimpses of the noon;
All this the nuptial guests beheld, and more:
Down either wall, in brackets deep embayed,
O'er-arched with looped-up curtains, statues stood
Of all the gods, with nichéd odour urns
Alternately between; high sculptured forms—
Boy Bacchus quaffing from a marble vase
A purple draught of vintage; Diana,
One foot upon the neck of a dead hart,
And Venus, with her fingers to her lips,
Kissing farewells to Adonis.   Beneath
Stood lion-footed tripods, ranged in tiers,
With braziers, lit with sandal-wood, at swing
Within their discs; whilst from the moulded roof,
A thousand lamps, pendent with chains of gold,
Through opal globes glimmered a deathless flame.
A row of altars, heaped with incense, smoked
On high amid the chancels; vested priests
Moved in the midst, and virgin choirs invoked,
With deep-breathed chants, the favour of the gods.
The rites performed, the revelry began;
A sound confused of whispered words arose,
The catch of harps, the gutt'ral hum of flutes,
The deep clang of oblationary cups.
The chamber filled—the whispered hum grew loud,
When, hark! ' Make way! the bride and bridegroom
    come.'—
The golden doors swung open—down the aisle,
Between the parted crowd, the lovers passed.
All lips grew still a moment, then a hail,
Loud as the shout of the unleashed typhoon,

Leapt from a thousand throats and shook the halls
Down to the deep foundations.   On they passed—
He, taller by a head than all his peers,
Moved stately as a god among the crowd ;
He'd doffed his hunting costume and appeared
A warrior prince of Greece—purple and gold—
His temples chapleted with branching bays,
Emblem of strength and beauty.   But all eyes
Were fixed upon the bride ; with crimson cheek
And down-dropped eye, leaning upon her lord—
O ! she was more than fair ; her shrinking limbs,
Smit by the rude gaze of a thousand eyes,
Blushed through her cassock, like the cloud-gowned
      moon ;
Her waist was girdled with a scarf of silk ;
And, braided with her curls, a coronal
Of pouting rose-buds blushed upon her brow.
' Hail, goddess ! hail !' the people cried, and strove
Who should bear in the richest crush of flowers
To strew along the path they were to tread ;
Until they moved knee-deep in flowers, flowers, flowers,
From sunny valleys in between the hills,
The glooms of ancient forests, and the brinks
Of precipices plucked, before the bee
Could creep into their closed-up honey cups—
Before the sun had put the dew-stars out.
Following in order due, with clinging robes
Of sea-green silk, the bride's shy sisters came.
O ! lovely as a garden full of flowers
Of every season and of every clime.
The smooth-faced pansy, and the home-bred broom,
Clematis drooping till its arms can cling
About the waist of some strong tower ; the rose
Conscious of queenly-hood, with curling lips,

Guarding its temple chastity with looks
That challenge but deny.

Be still ! be still ! Apollo takes the harp !
The Muses crowd around him ; all is hush.
With touch inspired, he spanned the thrillant strings
In prelude ; awhile, like a falling tear,
The music paused and trembled, loath to leave
Its home among the chords; then, like a lark,
That feels the nearing heaven upon its wings,
It gathered strength ! it rose ! it grew !—
It oversoared all bounds ! 'twas free ! 'twas free !
And panting, choking with the rush of heaven,
The breathless chords throbbed out the glory,
Rapt into incoherence with a rush
Of short gasping asphyxia notes that seemed
Almost to burst the spirit of the harp
To utter them.
Then, when the storm of song was at its height,
Sudden it turned—and fell—and sunk into
The querimony of a sigh—and ceased—
And left all hearts vibrating with the strain.
Then all the Muses broke into a song,
Apollo leading them :
‘ *Harps! harps! harps! Shall your chords be dumb ?*
  O ! dipt the lips in the reeling vine,
Thrilled through and through with the power divine,
  We come ! we come !’
     *   *   *   *   *
              Why linger we ?
The nuptial rites performed, the wedded pair,
Amid the shouts of men and gods, sat down
On thrones, 'twixt crouching dragon wings, beneath
The shadow of a tasselled canopy.
The site was lofty, and, from thence, the view

Compassed the farthest limits of the hall :
The teeming daïs ; the costly coverlets ;
And couches deep of quilted Tyrian
Buffed with the down of doves ; and heaped-up harps ;
And cups in pools of wine, upon the floor ;
And costly mats ; and stools with silver feet,
Plashed with the blood of quinces crushed to death ;
And broken bends of hymeneal wreaths ;
And trodden roses gasping out their sweets
Beneath the feet of movers to and fro.
The revelry grew louder ; all the gods
Ranged round the board, or lolled on golden thrones,
Spectators of the scene.   The wedded pair
Descended and assumed seats next the gods.
Rich was the feast : high foaming nectar cups,
And honey heaped in pitchers of cold stone ;
Cream foaming in the depths of icy wells,
And cisterns running o'er with flower-crowned wine.
Black slave boys passed the white-crowned cups about ;
A hundred damsels flitted to and fro
With silver, scented lavers for the guests ;
While naked slave girls with bejewelled hair,
And arms and ankles braceleted with gold,
Pursued the Maenad mazes of a dance
To the mad clash of castanets.
But hark ! a sound ! with an impatient burst
The doors swung open, and a female form,
With queenly robes and step imperial,
Swept down the hall ! and 'mid a hush profound,
With look of insupportable disdain,
Drew from her breast an apple of pure gold,
And whirled it down the banquet board.
Chink ! chink ! against the hollow cups it rang,
And passing by each dainty-laden dish,

And in and out the golden canisters,
Paused opposite the bride : ' For the most fair !'
The being cried, and turned and disappeared.
A tremor ran through every guest : each sought,
In other eyes, the meaning of a thing
That none might comprehend ; it came, 'twas gone—
Before the rough-jarred mind could form a thought,
The tongue a syllable, the sweep of robes,
The golden clangour of the closing door
Proclaimed the being gone.   What could it be ?
Was it a god ?   But lo ! the gods are here,
Guests of the wedding-feast ; was it a fiend—
A minion of the midnight Proserpine,
A blast-rid hag, half human and half hell ?
The golden fruit paused opposite the bride ;
Was it an omen ?   Let the priests be fetched !
Ho ! fetch the priests—what does the thing import ?
O ! what the mystical significance,
At such an hour of such a visitant !
Still lay the golden mystery on the board —
All eyes were fixed on it as by a spell,
But not a hand durst touch, till one more bold
Strode down the hall, picked up the shining orb,
Returned, and placed it in the hands of Jove.
With thoughtful brow the dreaded father took
And turned the golden apple in his hands ;
And ' *detur pulchriori*' read, low-breathed,
In lines deep graven on the crisped rind,
And ' *detur pulchriori*' read again,
Then turned and, lifting up his head, spake thus :
'That haughty mien, that lip of cold disdain,
That look of ill-suppressed malignity,
Are not, O sons of men, unknown to us
The dwellers of Olympus.   Oft when met

In heavenly synod or in purple rout,
That form intrudes, that voice is heard, that eye
Rests on the counsel, on the revel rests,
And concord is no more.   Yea, it is told
That in the very chamber of the bride
Her hated presence is not all unknown—
Eris, her name, the outcast of the heavens—
Yea, she it is who, uninvited, comes,
To wreak in hateful looks and ominous deeds,
'Mid men and gods, the vengeance of neglect.
But hark ! this only is the time of seed,
The harvest is not yet ; a little cloud
Has overcast the blue, the storm delays,
The thunder threatens, but is still withheld.
These things are not the growth of one short hour,
Ye see but the incipience of ill :
Her plots must shape, her purposes mature,
And though immortal eyes may see of all
An ominous sequel ; though immortal ears
May catch far off the presage of events
That may not be withstood ; though war should rage,
Though hosts should fall, though cities be o'erthrown,
These things shall not be yet.   Then why these fears,
These downcast looks, these tremblings of dismay ?
O ! rest beneath the vine : the winter wind
Is hardly known among the pine-woods yet ;
On with the feast ! let slip the Bacchic shout !
Strike, strike, ye bards, the smooth-lipped dulcimers !
Arise ! lift up your heads ! arise ! arise !
And in the full-grown dignity of men
Be greater than the god !'
                     So ended he.
And now once more the revelry grows loud ;
Once more was heard the careless clash of cups,

Once more the song, once more the harp aspired
The truly brave fear only the unknown ;
The thing revealed, the serpent spell is broke.
No trace was left upon a thousand brows
Of that which late had palsied every heart ;
The bold grew careless, and the careless bold—
Why tremble at a danger so remote ?—
The mystery is passed, the certainty
Is matter for their scorn.   Fill, fill the cups !—
The silver wine cistern has half way ebbed—
Bear in, ye slaves, bear in the bursting hides,
And ever as the mountained fruit grows less,
Ye maids bring in upon your toiling heads
Fresh baskets full, heaped even to the brims.

  * * * * *

    The lovers sat apart,
And watched the sport as though they saw it not.
Theirs was a love too deep for levity,
And spite the sworn assurance of the god,
A cloud has settled on the bride's white brow
That would not be dispelled ; and even he,
Who knew each shape that ever death assumed,
Was conscious of a feeling that had quenched
A happiness less perfect, less intense.
They talked in words unheard amid the din
But to the ear addressed.   She at his feet
Rested her head against his knee, while he
With fondling hand caressed the curls that fell
In gentlest undulations to his feet.
' And is your happiness complete ?' he said.
' Complete,' the maid replied, ' yet not complete :
I feel like one who, standing in the calm,
Yet sees the gathering clouds, and knows that soon
The tempest will descend.'   She spoke and sighed.

Then there was silence for a little space.
At length, as one who talks with her own soul,
Uncertain of the wisdom of her thoughts,
With still averted eyes the maid resumed :
' I know a cave among the sea-stained rocks,
Westward, 'twixt Phthia and Pharsalia.
I found it out one evening, long ago,
When, wearied from the festival of shells,
I'd parted from the nymphs, and wandered off,
To weep away in solitude the love
That even then was paining at my heart.
'Tis at the entrance of a vale that lies
'Twixt two the fairest of the Othryan hills.
Within, 'tis murmurous with the chime of springs,
That bubble up 'twixt crystal clefts, and then
Trickle away unseen into the sea.
I've furnished it with every sort of shell,
And, in an arch, there is a sort of couch,
That I have heaped with fragrant ocean flowers,
And all about it trained a vine that now
Hangs rich in fruit.   O ! 'tis a lovely spot,
And, from the hour I found it out has been
A secret known to few, or none, but me ;
Thither we'll go, and there unknown we'll dwell,
Until this threatened evil has gone by.'
' Aye ! thither, thither, when the feast is o'er,
We'll steal away unseen.   The vine-hung rock
Shall be our bridal couch ; the screaming gulls
Shall sing for us a ceaseless spousal hymn ;
And all day long we'll frolic in the foam,
Or, resting 'neath the rocks, recount again
How gods have loved, how goddesses been won.
And you shall lead me by the hand to where
The sea-birds build, the dolphin broods are caught,

And, in and out the hoarse wet caves, shall teach
My lips to tune the Triton shells ; my hands
To weave the samphire pods, and string the pearls,
To add new beauty to our cavern home.
O ! thither, thither, thither, we will go ;
And while the gathering clouds loom big with fate,
While out a lengthened marriage moon in all
The unforbidden luxuries of love.'

COPHETUA

Away, away ! must I forswear
  A greater love than can be told,
Because, forsooth, my temples bear
  A paltry rim of gems and gold ?
The very clown behind the plough
  Is free to choose his love—his bride,
Aha ! the crown may bind my brow,
  It shall not bind my heart beside ;
    I love, I love the beggar-girl,
      The beggar-girl, the beggar-girl ;
    I love, I love the beggar-girl,
      And I will marry her ! he cried.

Despite, despite the cynic saw,
  Oh ! it is more than half divine
To sit upon the lips of law,
  The ruler of a land like mine !
But, by the right of those sweet lips,
  A station at that sacred side,   .
They're light—aye, lighter than the chips
  Washed shoreward by the winter tide.

I love, I love the beggar-girl,
    The beggar-girl, the beggar-girl ;
I love, I love the beggar-girl,
    And I will marry her ! he cried.

No, no ! such chains shall never bind
    While I've the power to break them through ;
I have the passions of my kind,
    I'll have the privileges too !
And while I hold the beam of right,
    I never, never will be tied !
What ! shear the locks of those who fight,
    And chain the ankles of the guide ?
    I love, I love the beggar-girl,
        The beggar-girl, the beggar-girl ;
    I love, I love the beggar-girl,
        And I will marry her ! he cried.

I love her for her deep brown eye,
    Her winsome face so pure and good,
And that, that love alone can buy—
    The first deep love of maidenhood.
And though her robe be worn and thin,
    And though the rents be thick and wide,
They better show the charms within
    It were a very sin to hide.
    I love, I love the beggar-girl,
        The beggar-girl, the beggar-girl ;
    I love, I love the beggar-girl,
        And I will marry her ! he cried.

This, this is but the husk—the rind
    That wraps the inner golden seed ;
A queenly heart, a queenly mind,
    And she shall be a queen indeed.

Then let the high-born villain sneer,
   And let the loveless fool deride,
Truth is a nobler thing than fear,
   Love is a nobler thing than pride.
     I love, I love the beggar-girl,
       The beggar-girl, the beggar-girl ;
     I love, I love the beggar-girl,
       And I will marry her ! he cried.

THYRMIS.

>   'What shall I do? . . .
> Why should I not, had I the heart to do it,
> Like to the Egyptian thief at point of death,
> Kill what I love?—a savage jealousy
> That sometimes savours nobly.'
>   *Twelfth Night.*

THE desert sand gleamed hot and dry,
   Where worn, and faint, and pale, he lay,
Weltering in the mid-day heat,
   Watching the life-blood ebb away ;
No voice to soothe, no tongue to greet,
   No hand to close the stiffening eye,
While, faint and low, he did repeat
   Stray echoes of the life gone by.

'The stirrings of an inner power,
   The promise of a glorious name,
Voices that spoke to me aloud,
   All urged me on to deeds of fame ;
Yet was I scoffed and scorned and bowed,
   The by-word of each pampered boor,
My greatest curse that I was proud,
   My greatest crime that I was poor.

' But, self-secure, with hollow sneer,
 They tempted me to do my worst,
They thrust a dagger in my hand,
 And bade me use it if I durst :
Then, mad, I seized the proffered brand,
 And swore by yonder burning sphere,
I'd do the deed of their command,
 And buy my stolen manhood dear.

' I tasted freedom, and, unweaned,
 I quaffed the last all-glorious drain,
Nor legal threat, nor social ban,
 Could curse me back to bonds again ;
The deepest depths to deeper ran,
 I stood unfriended and unscreened ;
Who would have made me less than man,
 Alas ! have made me more than fiend.

' Then welcome death ! I've lived, I die
 As noblest hearts have lived and died ;
Unchecked in thought, uncurbed in deed,
 Unbroken in a lawful pride.
The debt is paid and I am freed,
 Then welcome death, again I cry,
I never cost the world a weed,
 I leave them nothing but a sigh.

Yet nothing ! Nothing did I say ?
 O God ! I've loved ! I've loved ! I've loved !
The fairest form, the sweetest mind,
 That ever lived and breathed and moved.
And must I leave such wealth behind
 To be a common harlot prey ?
No ; by the life I have resigned,
 Chariclea shall die to-day !'

He ceased, he raised his heavy eye,
   Whilst fast the life escaped his side,
And wildly tottering to the cave,
   He sought his queen, his love, his bride.
Oh ! strong to soothe though not to save,
   She comes ! She comes, and with a cry
Beholds the beautiful, the brave,
   Sink at her feet, to die, to die.

She bent above him ; tear on tear
   Mixed with the crimson stanchless tide ;
While he, with fevered fingers, seeks
   The gem-boss'd steel upon his side.
She chafed his hands, she kissed his cheeks,
   She breathed her sorrow in his ear,
The while, with love-learnt skill, she seeks
   To stay the life's too swift career.

Alas ! 'tis vain—'tis more than vain,
   His cup is full, his course is run ;
And even love's all-powerful art,
   Is weak against the Mighty One.
But lo ! a start, a sudden start,
   A mingled cry of joy and pain,
She clasps her lover to her heart,
   Slain on the bosom of the slain !

THE BIRTH OF A THOUGHT.

'A great thought strikes along the brain
And flushes all the cheek.'
TENNYSON.

I.

THERE is a spot among the gray slate cliffs
Where grows a knot of aged elms ; below,
Forsaken of the tides, a little cove
Gleams like a golden moon-bow ; and above,
In the veiled month of August, the low breeze
Whispers its secrets in the bended ears
Of the far nodding corn.   This tent of trees
Is pitched about mid-way between the two,
While to the right and to the left extend
The gray slate cliffs, enlightened here and there
By a hard patch of stunted blackberry bush.
It is a lovely spot as heart could wish :
A little rill gleams out among the ferns,
And drops down mossy stairs into the sea ;
And tonsured daisies deck the deep green floor
Through all the varied lapses of the year.
The earliest primroses and violets
Here open their wet eyes ; and the young bees
Hang at the nipple of the honeysuckle,
That bares its beauty to the first spring breeze.

II.

Hither, at noon, upon a long past day,
There came a youth whom all the Muses loved,
And stretching his tired limbs beneath the trees,
Surrendered every impulse of his soul
To beauty and to thought.

III.

The hours sped by unmarked; an open book
Lay on the grass beside him; but his eye
Had wandered from the page, and dwelt intent
Upon the scenes some fancy of the bard
Had whispered into being; the great sun
Had turned its glowing face toward the west;
The sea had left the little creek beneath,
And, in the distance, its low voice was heard
Mellowed to one long murmur; while at times,
Stirred by some wandering wind, the sleeping corn
Heaved a long-lingering sigh and slept again.
To right and left the gray unshaded cliffs
Stretched hot and arid 'neath the nervous glare
Of the full sun gaze; and the drowsy hum
Of myriad insect wings fell on his soul
Soft as a lullaby; but, with his eye
Concentrated upon far fairer scenes,
The poet was unconscious of them all.
He neither spake nor moved, he hardly breathed,
Save when at times he'd rise to catch the wings
Of some sweet, swift ethereal idea,
That like the crimson flutterings of a rose
O'er-blown before its peers, fell from the maze
Of fragmentary sounds and sights and scents
That formed the Paradise of his ideal.

IV.

Anon, his brow
Flushed with the travail of a larger birth;
A strange wild light that was not of the earth
Gleamed in the well-like darkness of his eye;
His nervous fingers worked as though with pain;

His heart beat quicker; and a dew, like stars,
Broke out beneath the cloud upon his brow.
In haste he rose, and pacing to and fro,
Broke down with rapid and unheeding tread
Hosts upon hosts of daisies; true, ah! true,
Though cold philosophy has slain the Muse,
And closed for aye the springs of Helicon,
The touch of some ethereal power was on him,
Enlivening and enlightening every sense.

v.

He paused; a pen—the midwife of the brain—
Was by to do his bidding; his lips moved
To the crude tune of those unnumbered notes
That lay about the avenues of speech,
Muffling the moon-like rising of his thoughts.
As one among the lute-chords seeks in vain
The key-note of a half-remembered song,
He swept the diapason of sweet words,
To catch the key-note of a strain that seemed
To pant upon the borders of expression.
The animated glance of his dark eye
Grew more intense; the hue upon his brow
Flushed into sunset deepness, and his heart
Beat—when,
As leapt the goddess from the brain of Jove,
So leapt, full statured and supremely god,
From out the poet's brain, the poet's thought.

*   *   *   *   *

And even so the vestal fire was lit;
The vestal fire of poetry and thought;
The vestal fire that never can go out.

THE DEATH OF BARBARA.

' My mother had a maid called Barbara ;
She was in love ; and he she loved proved mad,
And did forsake her ; she had a song of willow,
An old thing 'twas, but it expressed her fortune
And she died singing it.'
                                        Othello.

THE end is near ; I feel, I feel
    That death is stealing o'er me ;
The scenes I know and love so well
    Are fading fast before me ;
And I see the land where God doth dwell
    As through a golden glory.

But well-a-day ! I still must weep
    That all his vows should be so vain ;
Why did he drive the barb so deep,
    If but to pluck it forth again ?
Nay, rather why was I, poor maid !
So soon deceived, so soon betrayed ?

And yet he loved me : O ! how oft,
    When the dewy moon's revealing
Shed a silence from aloft,
    And the vesper bell was pealing,
He'd look into my eyes and say,
    With accents quivering with feeling,
' O ! without thee, my Barbara,
    My soul were sick beyond all healing !'

Then, smit with passion, he would start
    Up from my feet where he was kneeling,
And clasp me trembling to his heart,
    And seal his love with love's own sealing.
O ! hard indeed the heart would be,
    That could say nay to such appealing.

Sings.

And so she sat under a sycamore-tree,
Sing all a green willow,
O ! why, O ! why was he false to me,
Sing willow, willow, willow ;
My love was deep as the deepest sea,
And pure as earthly love could be,
Sing willow, willow, willow.

    *   *   *   *   *

Can I forget the hour when first
  He told me he did love me?
The strange new life that seemed to burst
  Around, within, above me?
The throb, the thrill—I feel it still ;
A love so great must come of ill,
  A love so deep must be accurst !

The summer moon came o'er the hill,
  The vale was hushed below,
Beside the stream that drives the mill,
  Three years ago, three years ago !
Ah me ! we were but children then,
  How swift the years do seem to go !

He told me tales of loves forlorn,
  Of knightly worth and maiden scorn ;
How heroes bold won wives of old
  With magic spear and golden horn ;
And then, with cheek as pale and cold
  As the moon that bent above,
He looked into my eyes, and told
  The fatal story of his love.

O ! cruel heart, is this, is this
  The love that then thy lips confessed me ?
Dost thou forget the long hot kiss
  Thou gav'st when first thy arms embraced me ?
O ! cruel heart, O ! cruel love,
  That curst me even whilst it blest me.

Sings.

I fondly dreamed his heart sincere,
  Sing all a green willow,
How would he murmur in my ear,
  Sing willow, willow, willow ;
And call me love, and call me dear,
His pride, his princess without peer,
  Sing willow, willow, willow.

*   *   *   *   *

Mad? mad?   The thought contains a balm
  That almost heals the wound away ;
Then maybe in his hours of calm
  He looks and longs for Barbara—
For the time gone by, when, arm-in-arm,
  We wandered in the wild wood-way,
And felt a charm beyond a charm,
  In all that love can do or say.

But well-a-day ! I dare not pray
  That such may be his fate ;
I dare not wish that mind away
  For love however great ;
Since fate decrees that we must part,
  What matter why or how ?
Be mine, be mine, the broken heart,
  Be his the cloudless eye and brow !

Sings.

If still he claims my latest thought,
 Sing all a green willow ;
If still I love, O ! blame me not,
 Sing willow, willow, willow.
Alas ! it is a common lot
To be beloved and be forgot,
 Sing willow, willow, willow.

Trusting, trembling—this alone
 Is woman's love, is woman's being ;
Drawn as by a magic stone,
 Ever drawn and ever fleeing.

How my poor bosom used to beat,
 When, down the garden-path, I caught
The well-known coming of his feet ;
And, like a spirit that doth meet
A death most welcome and most sweet,
 I fled from that which most I sought.

And yet I loved, and loved the more
 Because my love was mixed with fear ;
For love is strongest battled o'er
 By a Northern atmosphere.
O ! had he known the love I bore,
 Would he, could he, thus have left me ?
Gone, O ! gone for evermore,
 Love and life and all bereft me.

O ! if there were tears for the deepest woe,
 And sobs for the saddest sigh,
Then should my hot tears flow and flow
 Till their fount were dry.

But alas! alas, I cannot weep,
  The burning tears refuse to come ;
Mine is a sorrow all too deep,
  Mine is a sorrow all too dumb.

Let me sing that song again,
  The song I love, the sad, the sweet!
Sorrow-pain soothes sorrow-pain,
  As heat deadens heat :
I feel, I know the end is nigh,
  Once more I'll sing it ere I die.

Sings.

O riven hearts! O streaming eyes,
  Sing all a green willow.
Tears were but made for broken toys,
  Sing willow, willow, willow.

The voice grew faint, and then it ceased ;
  And as the cows came o'er the wold,
And as the moon looked up the east,
  And as the vesper tolled,
A spirit passed into its rest,
  Beyond the border-line of gold.

THE MOODS OF LAMECH HELZUDTHI.

I.

'I SAT alone by the midnight fire, that had sunken down
  to a clinking glow,
When the house was lapped in a leaden sleep,
  And the lamp was burning low.

' But my eyes were wide as the frozen stars that stared
    from heaven as the clouds flew by ;
    And my thoughts were wild as the outer wind
      That drove those clouds across the sky.

' For I brooded deep o'er a causeless wrong and a
    smooth-said taunt that I daren't return ;
    And my thoughts were wild as the outer wind,
      And my soul did burn, and my soul did burn.

' And the thrilling schemes of a mad revenge, and the
    killing words of a deep retort,
    And a sense of dependent impotence
      Were tossed like chips in the seeth of thought.

' And must I sheath my conscious strength with a humble
    blush and a low-bent head,
    When the words that leap to my bleeding lips
      Would beat him down like a bolt of lead ?

' "No ! no !" I cried, as the stinging thought touched like
    a goad on my burning brain,
    " I'll dare the brunt of his fiercest hate,
      And fling the taunt in his teeth again."

' Then back like some detested shape to the gaze of its
    parent Frankenstein,
    Came the chilling thought of the pit-eyed train,
      That waited the word of his risen spleen.

' But worse, far worse than the darkest deed of his pent-up
    hate or his practised rage,
    Was the chilling thoughts of the gifts and grace
      Of his serpent patronage.

'O ! this, this, this was the killing coil that I could not
    brook, that I dare not break,
      Though weak as the strand of the woven sand,
        Yet fast and firm as the folded snake.

' Then rose distempered questionings of how and why
    these things should be ;
      Why his should be the right to rule,
        Why I should bow to his decree.

II.

'O ! sad was the sound of the wind that night as it
    panted and pushed at the window pane,
      Or, locked in the arms of the staggering trees,
        Wrestled and writhed like a demon in pain.

' Then sinking away, away, away, it seemed to muse o'er
    its weight of woe,
      And its voice sunk down to a half-heard sob,
        Very low, very low ;

' Till the bitter thought of its grief and wrong swept back
    again o'er its half-eased mind,
      And it rose and roared through the rocking world
        In a passion dark and blind.

' And the double tick of the watch of death, hid where
    away it were hard to tell,
      Chilled and thrilled my sceptic heart
        Like the sound of a passing-bell.

III.

' Then I rose and took from the antique shelf, from the
    dust where they long had lain,
      The poets whose divinest songs
        Are those inspired by grief and pain.

' And many a sad-souled tale I read, and many a bitter
    song
        Of streaming eyes and heart-broke sighs,
            Of grief, neglect, and wrong ;

' Till my heart grew calm, and I mused and mused on a
    thousand thoughts of a thousand things,
        That only the spell of the midnight wind
            Or the midnight silence brings.

' And the past crept back, as when we hear the music of
    a far-off song,
        And the friends and the scenes of the days long
            dead,
            Arose again in a life-like throng.

' And I wandered again in the moss-matted lane where
    the dog·rose blushed 'mid the guardant thorn,
        And away, away o'er the far-stretched heaths
            Of the village where I was born.

' And down by the stream that drove the mill when the
    sluice was up and the wet wheel flew,
        And deep in the shade of the pine-tree woods,
            Where the pigeons built and the bilberries grew.

' Then my thoughts went on and on and on, into the
    night of the great unknown,
        When all that I love shall be scattered or dead,
            And O ! I shall be alone, alone !

' Like a city's lamps as the mid of night sinks down on the
    busy scene,
        They faded away, they faded away,
            Till scarcely one was seen.

'But worse to me than the pang of death was the close of
      each well-loved eye ;
    Death's only death to those who're left,
       'Tis life to those who die.

'Then I rose, for my heart was calm, and each passion
      was turned to prayer,
    And I felt a love for all mankind,
      And bless'd them unaware.

'O human heart ! O human heart ! who, who shall rule,
      shall fathom thee,
    O ! wayward as the clouds thou art,
      O ! deeper than the sea.'

EGOISMS.

'MUCH STUDY.'

THERE was a time when all things were to me
    A mystery and a delight ; the gleam
Of the cold moon ; the sun, the sky, the sea,
    Were things too sacred to be made the theme
Of daring and familiar questionings ;
    But time arrived when to my heart, all pale,
    There stole a hunger to tear down the veil,
And search into the very soul of things :
    From that unhappy moment I began
To sound the seas of thought ; to pant and pore,
From midnight unto midnight, over lore
    Deep hidden from the common eye of man ;

But what the profit? what strange, new domains
   Have opened to the ever-roving glance?
Alas! the only harvest of our pains
   Is surer knowledge of our ignorance.

THE SOURCES OF SONG.

I.

It hath been said of poets that they learn
   Their chiefest songs in sorrow; that the spheres
Alone may rival with the notes that burn,
   Fierce and resistless, in the wake of tears.
It may be; but to me the dreams that throng
   About a heart at peace, the all-serene
   Of Nature and of life, have ever been
The richest and the purest founts of song.

The solitude that dwells among the hills;
   The voice of lonely streams; the sea-gulls' cry
Upon the twilit beach; the happy bells   ·
   That wake the marriage morn; the summer sky—
Yea, all things good, or beautiful, or grand,
   Speak to me in a language which, though hard,
At times impossible, to understand,
   A language that I dare not disregard.

II.

The songs of Greece; the leafiness of June;
   Midnight and music on a summer main;
Dreams of the years gone by; the haunting moon
   Among the ruined walls of shrine or fane;
The low of cattle coming o'er the lea
   At toll of vesper bell; a sudden glimpse,
   Around the point of some lone shore, of nymphs
Just stripping for a frolic in the sea;

The power of Truth; the love of womankind;
  The gracefulness of youth; the strength of men;
The thrill of freedom when a wakened mind
  Arises and shakes off the tyrant's chain;
The sorrow of an ancient poesy,
  Conned in the twilight, by a forest stream—
These, these my muse delights in; these shall be
  Henceforth my inspiration and my theme.

III.

But who assumes the poet-voice, and sings
  Of moods and feelings he has never known;
Who apes an inexperienced grief, and wrings
  From every joy, a murmur or a groan;
Who, blinded to the sun's majestic blaze,
  Sees but the spots upon his disc; to whom
The poet's fire is but the phosphos haze
  That trembles in the region of the tomb—
With such the poet has nor lot nor part;
  Intruders on the king's highway of song,
And false alike to Nature and to Art,
  Their feeble pipings cannot charm us long:
True heart-grief is too sacred to be made
  The motto of a pennon; they alone
Would have their bosom publicly displayed
  Who never knew a sorrow of their own.

IV.

Enough, enough! Shall he whose soul is lit
  Bright with the vestal planet-light of song
Court sorrow for the sake of singing it,
  And die of an imaginary wrong?

No desert-voice is his, to dwell apart
   And sing of moods exclusively his own ;
He is an echo of the great world-heart—
   The voice of all that it has felt and known ;
And while the world runs round on golden wheels,
   And every eye has glimpses of the gods,
   And while the axe is hidden in the rods,
And with the poison is the balm that heals—
Away, away, these hopeless threnodies !
   The owl has ceased, the lark is on the wing—
Sweets with the bitters, laughter with the sighs:
   God loves us all ; heaven's over everything.

THE VOICE OF GOD.

' Arise ! arise ! O poet ; press thy ear
   Against the cold breast of the world, nor start
To hear the music of thy parent sphere,
   And count the mystic beatings of her heart ;
For Nature must have poets ; every flower
   Is full of latent music, and demands,
   With motion eloquent as claspèd hands,
A heart to feel, a tongue to give it power.'

I raised my head ; there was no fair form near,
   The voice had ceased, the message seemed com-
      plete ;
Only the winter woods were in the rear,
   Only the winter sea was at my feet ;
But straight I rose (I dare not disobey),
   And swore to tread the path that Shakespeare
      trod.
These sounds heard in the silence—what are they ?
   The voice of Inspiration and of God !

FROM TWO STANDPOINTS.

I.—GIVE ME THY CHILD.

As flows the stream through plain and plot,
    'Twixt primrose banks, o'er leaf and lea,
Nor thinks, nor dreams of higher lot
    Until it sights the distant sea ;
So moves the stream of loves and fears,
    Pleased with the scenes 'mong which it rose,
Until the winding water nears
    The depths of love to which it flows.

Once in the bosom of the sea,
    Farewell, farewell to plot and plain !
So flows her love from you to me,
    And shall it, can it turn again ?
Go, bid the rabid Nile obey,
    Compel the Tigris with a thrall ;
But let the rush of love have way,
    Or it will burst and ruin all.

What power or privilege is thine
    To sway the purpose of her hand ?
The right divine, of love like mine,
    Is not to crave but to command.
Her heart already is my own—
    'Tis yours, 'tis yours for which I sue.
O ! who would drag the muds of Rhone
    To win the gems of Cesinu ?

Ay, ay ! frown on, until your frown
    Darkens the coming of the day ;
A frown may fright a fancy down,
    Love never yet was frowned away.

Indeed, if might were king of right,
  'Tis I should frown, 'tis you should sue ;
And e'en though right should govern might,
  I have a higher claim than you.

I will not dwell with pedant phrase
  Upon her charms, for O ! for O !
How far they mock all words of praise,
  You, more than I, must feel and know.
To call her good would be to call
  The sunshine bright, the lily fair.
I love ! I love ! and that is all
  The worth, the wisdom of my prayer.

By right of love, all rights above,
  Her heart is yours, the first and nighest ;
When love is overbid by love,
  The boon is his who bids the highest.
And can you still be deaf and cold
  To reason's claims and passion's prayers?
The sin's the same, of those who hold
  And those who take what is not theirs.

' Who'll buy ? who'll buy ?'—this, this, the cry ;
  ' A pretty maid upon the mart !
A lordling's land secures her hand '—
  A double damn upon her heart,
High honour sold for goods and gold,
  Great Nature's landmarks overthrown :
She sighs for love, you offer land,
  She asks a loaf, you give a stone !

Love cannot act beneath the rose,
  'Tis open as the sun in shining ;
You say you love, you yet oppose
  The boon for which she most is pining !

'To love, and yet to love to let'—
  You know the adage worn and wise—
Unless the act approve the fact,
  Who says he loves, I say he lies.

II.—WED WHOM THOU WILT.

That hand is bold that seeks to hold
  The swelling wind, the risen foam;
Away! the text is dead and cold
  That says that love begins at home!
For this we plan, and plant, and ply,
  Slow toiling on from sun to sun:
An idle boy comes smiling by,
  And all our labour is undone.

Ay, love! but say, did ever love
  Add food or fuel to store or stone?
Although you're wed, you must be fed,
  You cannot live by love alone.
A truce to Greeks and Grots and Groves!
  Such suit not with the colder West;
The weddings of the loves and loaves
  Are aye the brightest and the best.

So near allied are love and pride,
  You're tost and lost between the two;
Because he smiled, because he sighed,
  He is, forsooth, in love with you.
O! when will youth attend the truth
  That age and wisdom would impart?
His care has touched your girl conceit,
  And straight you deem it is your heart.

But go ! old times have passed away ;
    The child directs, the sire must bow ;
And yet the brides of that old day
    Loved, and were loved, as much as now.
But go ! but go ! 'tis even so,
    The flower is plucked, the root must die ;
Mine, mine is but to feel and know
    That you were mine in days gone by.

EREMOPSIS.

FAIR was the scene,
Yet destitute of those soft sights and sounds
Component of a poet-artist's dream :
No wood from out whose shade the bluebell glimpse
Breaks like a chasm in a summer cloud ;
No stream at struggle in the matted fern,
Or bush alive with bird-songs and the hum
Of honey-hunting bees, was there ; but rocks—
Rocks tumbled into heaps and ivy lashed,
And mine-shafts nettled o'er with spider webs,
And scraps of broken tools, and ruined huts ;
And reaching from the niches of the rocks,
And slipping half-way down the broken shafts,
Sea-pinks, blushing and bowing in the breeze.

But the most striking feature of the place
Was a low tower, close down beside the sea ;
What hand erected it, or what its use,
Its date, its origin, its history,
Were things at once untalked of and unknown.

For whispered tales about the midnight hearth,
Of forms with sheeted heads and dragging chains,
And howls and oaths heard high above the storm,
Made it a theme forbidden in those parts.

In autumn, at the setting of the sun,
I sat within the shadow of that tower;
The great red wheel had reached the end of heaven,
And, flushed and far, the sea stretched out beneath,
Beating and bleeding like a wounded heart.
I read, until the light began to fade,
An ancient tale, that taught with many words
The charms and influences of solitude.
Much worn and torn the volume was withal;
An old, old thing, a simple thing, and yet
Not destitute, 'mid much of little worth,
Of happy gleams of nature and of truth;
One I remember in particular:
' What charms hath solitude to him who feels
The early promptings of a first-born love,
Yet doth not know for what his spirit craves!
Upon the willowed banks of some still stream,
Far in the shadow of an ancient wood,
In silent lanes, and on the moonlit beach,
Beings that claim a kindred with his soul
Do visit him.'   I read the passage twice,
Then paused and thought upon the truth of it,
And thought and thought upon the truth of it,
Until, somehow, the spirit of the theme,
And that sweet sense of sadness that is meet
To render loveliness the most complete,
Seemed stealing like a shadow over me;
And soon, yet half unconsciously, I strayed
Close to the entrance of the gate of dreams.

The red light of the sun; the beating breeze;
The distant dipping of a fisher's oar;
The cold lap of the waves; the weird old tower;
The wheeling and the wailing of the gulls,
Blended confusedly with thoughts, and things
Long since esteemed forgotten, formed themselves
Into a dream, chaotically fair.
These scattered fragments soon began to close
Around one central object, which partook
Of all the loveliness of all the rest,
And left them all the lovelier for the theft.
I looked; it seemed to be a maiden form,
O'er whose transparent limbs was flung a veil,
Wrought like a Grecian stole.   She did not speak,
But stood bare-footed in the dream-like flowers,
And gazed upon me like a startled fawn,
While through the rosy cleft of half-shut lips
Her breath escaped in short warm throbs, and one white
    hand
Held back the weight of deep down-drooping curls.
Wildly I started in my dream or trance
Into a deeper and a deeper bliss.
A sense of swooning awe stole over me:
I saw, I felt, I knew it was the form,
It was the breath, it was the eye of Love!
And like a very pagan sinking down,
I worshipped and I wept.
       *   *   *   *   *
I do not know how long the trance continued,
But all the listening stars were wide awake,
And the still moon was high, when life crept back
With all its passionless realities.
The book I had been reading still was near,
And by the silent light of all the stars

My eyes at waking fell upon these words:
' What charms hath solitude to him who feels
The early promptings of a first-born love,
Yet doth not know for what his spirit craves !
Upon the willowed banks of some still stream,
Far in the shadow of an ancient wood,
In silent lanes, or on the moonlit beach,
Beings that claim a kindred with his soul
Do visit him !'

I rose and shook away the clinging dew,
And with slow steps walked homeward through the corn

* * * * *

Since then I oft have visited that spot,
Hoping that I might see that form again ;
But though the blessed vision cometh not,
Yet doth the memory of the form remain,
And like the picture of a virgin fair
Graven on some cathedral window-pane,
No time can alter, and no change impair,
The image printed on my heart and brain,
Until the stone of death shall shiver it amain.

THE LOVE AFFAIRS OF PHILANDER PADISCO.

I.

O ! POWER of Love ! and O ! unhappy he
Who, in an hour of proud self-strength, hath sworn
To break the bonds the mightiest have borne,
And, nobly seeming, be ignobly free ;

Bitter the penance that his soul shall feel,
    When, great with wrath, the offended god shall rise
And drag the boaster at his chariot wheel,
    Weeping and wounded, in a thousand eyes.

Alas! the crime is mine: with proud lip curled,
    And scorn that bordered on the sense of hate,
I dipped into the Styx they call the world,
    And madly dreamed I was invulnerate.

But thou didst smile! Swift, swift, through every vein
    Sped the mad fire I never could conceal;
Storm as I might, the galling truth was plain,
    My head was weaker than Achilles' heel.

II.

There is a twofold character in love:
    The first and greatest is the love we bear—
A sense of dread and longing that doth move
    Within and from our spirit like a prayer.

The other is the love that we impart—
    A reflex passion that that soul conceives,
That gazes too intently on a heart
    Made conscious of the ecstasy it gives.

This is the cause of all a lover's pain—
    An aching void of unfulfilled desire;
That, like a charm, heals up the wound again,
    And makes the life's capacity entire.

Alas! the love that kills has smitten me;
    But turn again that hope-reviving eye,
And, like the son of Auga, I shall be
    Cured by the weapon of whose wound I die!

III.

Alas for him whose heart has loved too well !
   She looked, she smiled, she sighed—it was enough ;
   Forthwith, unthinking, from such flimsy stuff,
I built me up a gorgeous citadel

Stuffed full of hopes and dreams as it would hold,
And there, like Ptolemy in days of old,
I inly swore my queen of love should dwell,
Unseen, inviolate, impregnable.

But, ah ! too late ! that smile so soft and bland,
   The languid heaving of that amorous sigh,
Proved darkly treacherous as Syrtisan sand,
   And poison as the air of Aconi.

Then, great with indignation, I arose,
   And smote the fabric I had reared, and swore,
By all the pain a wounded spirit knows,
   I'd never trust the love of women more.

'O ! WHERE THE PATH JUST DIPS AND TURNS.'

O ! WHERE the path just dips and turns,
   Before it bursts upon the leas,
He saw her 'mong the flowers and ferns,
   Upon a bank beneath the trees.
Her feet were splashing in the brook
   That tipped the forest's fretted rim,
But, e'er he reached her, she forsook
   Her pastime, and drew near to him ;
     But 'twasn't that, 'twasn't that.

Her kirtle, void of loop or hook,
  Rustled in ribbons to her knees ;
Her lap was full of hazles, shook
  In sunburnt bunches from the trees.
And O ! more maddening than the cup,
  Deep drunk beneath the Rhenish dew,
In haste she caught the apron up,
  And caught—and caught—the kirtle too !
    But 'twasn't that, 'twasn't that.

'In sooth,' he cried, 'a sweeter sight
  I have not seen for many a day !
Forbid, forbid, that I should fright
  The pretty water-nymph away !'
She said—and drooped her curly head
  To hide the blush she scorned to own—
She said—he knew not what she said ;
  He dwelt upon the voice alone !
    But 'twasn't that, 'twasn't that.

Her eyes were of the deepest brown,
  Tressed in by lashes dark as night,
That, curling up and curling down,
  Pressed all the witchery into sight ;
And streaming from her puckered hood,
  O ! wondrous wealth of bright and black !
Her untied curls in one great flood
  Floated in folds adown her back ;
    But 'twasn't that, 'twasn't that.

A charm—a deeper charm than lies
  In country bloom or city skill,
That dwelt about her lips and eyes,
  Unconscious of its power to kill :

A charm—a charm without a name ;
   A thing unsought, unbought, unbid,
That seen, or secret, wrought the same
   On everything she said and did—
     'Twas that, 'twas that !

SILENCE AND DEATH.

I.

NATURE is never still : when all around,
   Hushed as a dreaming maiden, seems to sleep,
Intent, we catch a soul-like under-sound,
   A lower life, a deep beneath a deep ;
The drone of wings ; the motions of the breeze ;
   The echo-breath of hollow and of hill—
These never cease ; the wilderness hath these !
   These, these are heard, though all things else are
     still.

II.

But if a moment there befall
An utter silence over all,
The calm that sleeps beneath the pall ;
Then Silence' self the void doth fill,
   She hath a music of her own,
   A tingling sound, a bell-like tone
The faintest breath hath power to kill.

III.

Can Silence be, and there be Life ?
   Sworn foes are they, the poet saith,
And Death alone can end the strife,
   For Silence is twin brother unto Death.

BEAUTY

O ! THERE is much of beauty upon earth ;
  In every land beneath the sun 'tis seen,
  The gift alike of mighty and of mean,
The mask of wickedness, the mark of worth.
Yea, there's some lineament in every face
  Of that Divinity that bent above
The yet unliving parent of our race,
  And breathed him into life and into love.
And it must be : for Beauty cannot die ;
  Despite of influences that debase,
  And time that would disfavour and deface,
It lives the all in all beneath the sky.
The liveliest evidence of God on earth,
  Can beauty fade, can beauty pass away ?
  No ! God Himself shall save it from decay,
And every age renew it from its birth.

A CRITICISM.

'TIS but the shrieking of the pegs,
  Ere yet the harp is fully strung ;
But there's the eye, the heart, the ear,
  And time shall bring the poet's tongue.

E'en now, though cramped in rhymes and rules,
  And struggling through a husky throat,
I seem at scattered times to hear
  A voice of more than common note.

The glitter of a golden wealth,
  Half hid in heaps of hueless ore,
The prelude of as sweet a song
  As ever charmed the world before.

For thought with truth, and truth with thought,
  Apt keynotes of the noblest song,
The one in two, the two in one,
  To thee abundantly belong.

Then break the bond of useless rule,
  The laws, the saws, of ancient date :
Be free ! O ! swear thou wilt be free ;
  For to be free is to be great.

No faery myths, no crude ideals—
  A heart to feel, an eye to see—
Be thine the poetry of *life*,
  Which is the life of poetry !

The way to do is the right to do ;
  Thou hast the right—the way is found !
Then take and tune the harp anew ;
  Thou'rt worthy, and thou shalt be crowned.

BRITISH SONG.

More flimsy dreams, by Eastern streams !
  More ghebirs, gondolas and galleons !
Is there no beauty upon earth
  But that of Spaniards, Turks, Italians ?

Enough ! enough ! such flimsy stuff
　　Had better far be left unwritten ;
To cheer and charm a British heart,
　　Your song must be a song of Britain.

O ! sing your own dear cottage home—
　　The windows blinded with the roses ;
The closes where the cattle roam ;
　　The cattle roaming in the closes ;

And if you fain would add a strain
　　Of higher beauty to your verses,
There's many an English Mary Jane
　　Fair as the Zelicas of Persis.

Sing these ! sing these ! until you fill
　　All earth and heaven with their praises ;
Then sing them o'er again, until
　　Your soul is gone in luscious phrases.

What ! leave your own rich shores to seek,
　　In foreign seas, a fancied jewel ?
Leave Greek to speak the praise of Greek,
　　He'll do it better far than you will !

—　—

SOMETHING NEW.

What shall I write ? what shall I write ?
　　Is all the poet's care and cue,
As night and day, and day and night,
　　He racks his brain for something new.

Ye must not sing of Love or Fame,
   The Sun, the Spring, the Sea, the Dew ;
A thousand bards have writ the same,
   And ye must give us something new.

The olden tales, of golden times,
   Of Gods and Greeks, or false or true,
Would damn the best of modern rhymes :
   We must, we must have something new !

The real ! the real ! this, this the cry
   Raised by the whole book-badgering crew ;
Romance—it is an ancient lie !
   Give us the real, give us the new !

Give us a legend of the street,
   A city song of ninety-two !
Not meet ! the devil is not meet !
   It must be meet if it is new.

Nature, whose pictures used to please,
   Is done to death—worn through and through ;
Then give us her deformities ;
   These, these, at least, are something new !

What matter though your rhymes are hard,
   And ragged as a beggar's shoe ?
Thou shalt be deemed a mighty bard
   If they contain the something new.

ESTRANGED.

THOUGH years have passed since last I dwelt
　　Upon the music of thy voice,
It still has power to soothe and melt,
　　And still I hope, and still rejoice.

A jealous thought, a hasty word,
　　And love had fled, and life was changed;
Too late we learned how deep we'd erred,
　　How mean the cause that had estranged.

Come back! come back! the past is dead;
　　Our love survives, our hearts are free;
Come ere the bloom of life has fled—
　　Come back, come back, to love and me!

———

TOO BEAUTIFUL.

I CANNOT hope, I dare not think;
　　'Twere fate to dream that thou wert mine.
What heart so bold as dare to drink
　　A cup so maddening, so divine?

Yea, there are moments when the heart
　　Could almost wish thee mean or vile;
Wert thou less heavenly than thou art,
　　E'en I were worthy of thy smile.

Thou art too good, too fair, too pure;
　　Love is thy due; but to possess,
What choicest spirit could endure!
　　The hope were heaven—the thought excess!

The least desire would desecrate,
   The faintest hope would be profane ;
But spirits still may contemplate,
   Though hands are powerless to attain.

THE RIVALS.

THE TIME AND THE PLACE.

THE fitful flail of an autumn gale
   Had threshed the forest's shockèd sheaves,
And everywhere through the misty air
   Faltered and fell the winnowed leaves.
The day had closed its bloodshot eye
With a lidless blink in the western sky,
And night came down like an empty pall,
   Its dark warp shot with a driving sleet,
Rolling and wrapping the earth withal,
   Wrapping the earth in a winding-sheet.

Maybe there gleamed in the heaven afar
The maiden moon and the mateless star ;
But never a rift or a rent was left,
For their leaking light, in the misty weft.

Such was the hour, the neighbourhood,
The margin of a rock-based wood.
The thronging trees were bare and bent,
Drawn up on the line of the rocks' descent ;
Below, below, like a jaded steed,
A river rolled ' with its wintry speed,'

Whose winding waters did divide
The forests piled on either side,
As though, of old, some mighty hand
Had cleft in twain the knitted land,
And flung the sullen stream between,
To guard the ominous ravine,
There, like a watchman, to remain,
To see they ne'er unite again.

And o'er the torrent's misty bed,
  Among the sheltering firs confined,
A lonely mansion reared its head,
  Far from the homes of humankind :
A darksome hour, a darksome scene,
But darker still the tale, I ween.

HERMIONE.

A chamber, whose receding pane
  Looked out upon the waste of night ;
A lamp suspended by a chain,
  Cutting a path of misty light ;
A crucifix in yonder nook,
  Low there, a silken-slashed settee,
Upon the daïs a claspèd book
  A claspèd book of poetry.

And lovely as the lipsome bloom
  That tinct' the first-born of the Springs,
Her hair, fresh from the silkworm's loom,
  Inweaving with the slender strings,
Bent o'er a lute, a female form
Sate, as though listening to the storm.

But O ! her thoughts were far away
    From the wild warfare of the wind,
For Fancy, wandering astray,
    Had left the present all behind ;
Even her lute neglected lay,
For 'twas the eve of her wedding-day.

Yet, like a warning, in her breast,
    There was a voice she could not still,
That robbed her spirit of its rest
    With whispers of impending ill,
An unexplained presentiment,
Foreshadowing some dark event.

She saw the cup, untasted yet,
Shivered to fragments at her feet,
And though she could not well foresee
How such a circumstance could be,
A vision and a voice revealed
    To inward eyes and inward ears,
What, though to outward sense concealed,
    Oppressed her with a thousand fears.

Now rising with a sudden start,
She pressed the lute against her heart,
And with its soothing sweetness sought
To dissipate the gloomy thought ;
In vain ! the pluckèd chords reply,
In echoes to her saddest sigh.
Then to the tinkle of the strings
She sings.

A simple song—a song that well
    Expressed her thoughts, relieved her breast ;
Ah ! music, music, those who tell
    Their story simplest, tell it best ;

Upyielding to its soothing spell,
Like a tired dove, she seeks her nest:
O Queen of dreams, be kind! be kind!
Steal all dark thoughts from Hermione's mind.

JEALOUSY.

Serena, sitting at her chamber pane,
Gazed out upon the darkness; her white arm
Rested upon the lattice, and her chin,
Sunk in the socket of her palm, upheld,
As on a column of wrought ivory,
Her aching head; for O! her heart was heavy;
A tear hung in the darkness of her eye
Like the lone moon at midnight; and a cloud,
Too, too significant of inward storms,
Loomed, thunder-threatening, along her brow.
Her heart was heavy; unbeloved, she'd loved
The self-same object of her sister's love
With all the ardour of her heart, and now,
With feelings that she dare not analyze,
Beheld, successless, a success
Bought with the price of her own happiness.

Anon she rose, and with a rapid step
Paced the low-roofed room, as though she sought,
By the swift motions of her burning limbs,
T'out-strip the rival swiftness of her thoughts;
But, like the memory of a crime, unknown
To all except the life on which it feeds,
Still, still they clung to her; and like a hart
That bears upon its side the fangèd sleuth,
Blinded with fear and pain, she hurried on,

Seeking the more to dissipate her grief,
Finding the more, in nursing it, relief.
A cold dew stood upon her brow ; the tear
That glittered in the midnight of her eye,
Moonlike, had caught the sunblaze of her passion ;
And over her white brow, like a torn cloud
Above a snow-crowned height, curled the dark
　　depths
Of her dishevelled hair ; her lips disclosed
To the soft passage of some muffled words,
Of which the final syllables alone
Were audible :
　　　'I must—the deed brooks no delay ;
　　　To-morrow is her wedding-day ;'
Whereon the bell tolled out the hour of midnight.

She paused, and, opening the chamber door,
Stood gazing, with a beating heart, adown
The silent corridor.　How densely dark !
Dark as the tomb of the departed midnights !
　　But her imagination peoples it
With thousand images, that flit and dance
In an unearthly maze before her eyes ;
She heard the storm, like a benighted bird,
Beating its wings against the window-pane ;
She felt the cold breath of the mouldering walls
Blow chill upon her temples, and again,
Closing the door, she slipped into the darkness.

A COUNTRY WEDDING-DAY.

The broad sun leapt upon his mountain throne,
And, planting one foot on the tempest's neck,
Crushed out its rebel life ; then with quick march,
Urging his banners to its utmost bound,
Installed himself the monarch of the world.

No purple pomp, no strained display,
Attend a country wedding-day.
Like forest streams, whose neighbouring song
Each has cheered each, the way along,
Late meeting in a lonely grot,
To man unknown, by man unsought,
Fulfil the vows by song-signs plighted,
And urge their common course united—
E'en as the wedding of the tides,
Are country maids made country brides.

Lo ! where the bending sky just tips,
The distant hills' uplifted lips,
In rustic finery, appears
A throng of distant villagers.

The raindrops flashed, as though the night
    Had dropped the stars upon the plain ;
And, in the eagerness of flight,
    Forgot to pick them up again ;
So bright they were, but doubly bright
    The sight of yonder maiden train.
The blush that, like a half-blown rose,
Wants but a zephyr to unclose ;

The artless looks that would conceal
The joys those very looks reveal;
Eyes bright as Hero's lamp, to guide
Some lone Leander to their side ;
Their hooded hair, like some sweet nun
   In forced celibacy confined,
Pent from the kisses of the sun,
   And from the cuddle of the wind ;
Except where, like the moss-curled nest,
   'Neath some cool bank, the wild wren weaves,
The scattered fringes peep confest
   From out the wimple's shady eaves.

Nor do their rustic robes suppress
All of their secret loveliness :
Short sleeves betray the buxom charms
Of sunburnt hands and sunburnt arms;
Skirts, ·halting 'twixt a double fear—
Will little or too much appear ?—
Betray the alternating views
On rosy feet of rustic shoes,
With half the lengths of knitted hose,
White as the secrets they enclose ;
Simplicity ! simplicity !
How little is there left of thee !

But whither away so blithe and gay ?
O ! Hermione's wedding-guests are they.

DEATH.

A shriek of woe, a sound of dread,
　　Pierces the morning like a dart.
'O ! Hermione is dead, is dead,
　　'Stabbed with a dagger to the heart !
Her shroud, her sheet—her bier, her bed:
O ! Hermione is dead, is dead !'

　　*　　　*　　　*　　　*　　　*

Who needs the aid of laboured lines,
　　Fettered with figures, tried and trite,
To learn that, when the morning shines,
　　The earth is beautiful and bright ?
And when the sullen night sinks down,
　　The brake, the tree, the flower, the grass,
All things partaking of its frown,
　　Are blended in a dusky mass.
Ah ! woe is me, the day is dead,
And darkness governs in its stead.

AN EVENING IN SPRING.

The youthful year
Had left the swaddling snow of cradle-time,
And, with the blush of conscious maidenhood,
Assumed its first ill-fitting finery.
Already the bright earth had half forgot
The cold death-struggle of its ancient king,
The rude unlawfulness of infant rule,
And watched, with a pleased smile, the ripening days

Of the sole scion of the line of Time.
Still, at uncertain intervals, untamed,
The rude mobility of homeless blasts,
Disbanded o'er the grave of the late year,
Gathering the remnant of their scattered tribe,
Swept in wild tumult o'er th' unconscious land,
As though they would dethrone its maiden monarch,
And bring again the latter lawlessness.
But now the whole green earth was still.
  The moon, like Ceres' reaping-hook,
    Hung crescent in the western sky;
  Afar the unrolled stream partook
    Of the silver of her eye.
The twinkling passage seemed to be
Like a fallen galaxy;
And, flashing in the argent light,
Each star became an aerolite.
A brood of stars was nestling
Beneath the Night's maternal wing;
And, on the earth, the far-fall'n dew
    Flashed in those stars' ten thousand rays,
Like the breastplate of the priestly Jew
    'Neath the Shekinah's mystic blaze.

AVAL.

There was a path among the trees
  That thronged the margin of the rock,
But so grown o'er with bilberries,
  And tangled fern, and hollyhock,
That the worn way was scarcely seen
'Neath such a wilderness of green.

'Twas beaten by the foresters,
Back in the half-forgotten years ;
But now no foot but of the hare
Disturbed the wild-flowers growing there,
Nature had chosen it to show
    How fair and fruitful she can be,
Without the aid of spade or hoe,
    Where no one toils and tills but she.

Yet on the night that I have said,
    Here wandered, weary and alone,
A youth—the youth who was to wed
    The fair and faithful Hermione.

He'd nowhere definite to go,
But wandered idly to and fro,
With folded arms and bended head,
Dreaming of her—the dead, the dead.

Six months had winged their leaden flight,
Six months, since that all-fatal night—
That night of all the year beside,
The night that robbed him of his bride.

What hand performed the fatal deed
    Was still unguessed of and unknown,
Though whispering gossips half agreed
    It was the hapless maiden's own ;
' For lack of love to him,' they said,
' Her sire had bid that she should wed.'

But, those, who knew the maiden, knew
    Her love was choice, her choice was free,

And that the youth—O ! who more true,
　More loyal, more chivalrous than he ?
There was a secret yet unsealed,
A mystery yet to be revealed.

So wandered he, with downcast head,
Dreaming of her—the dead, the dead.
But lo ! where'er his soft steps stray,
A silent figure dogs his way ;
But when he, wondering, stopped to see
What curious being it might be,
With startled look and nervous tread,
Silent and swift, it turned and fled.

Sure none but one whose soul was torn
By passion, or a keener thorn,
At such an hour, would seek alone
A spot so wild, so weird, so lone !
' 'Tis but a shade—an apparition
Of fancy born, or superstition,'
He said, and on his way once more
Strolled deep in musings as before.

Again he turns, and there again
The figure stands distinct and plain
And, by the moon's enchanted light,
He sees that it is clad in white—
A moment stands, and then it flees
Into the shadow of the trees.

Could a mere phantom of the mind
Assume a form so well defined ?
Could——

A feeling of delightful dread
   Shot, like an arrow, through his brain :
O ! could it be the dear and dead
   Returned to visit him again ?
With beating heart and tiptoe-tread,
He neared the spot where it had fled,
When lo ! half hidden by the trees,
A form—a female form—he sees.

She did not fade, she did not fly,
But fixed on him a large dark eye ;
Then with a start, a cry, a bound,
Leapt out into the open ground,
And flung herself upon her knee
At Aval's feet imploringly.

Amazed, he marked the prostrate maid,
Or marked, at least, a maiden's shade ;
.Was that the form his dreams had given
The life, the lineaments of heaven ?
Was that the pure, the peerless one ?
Was that his lost love Hermione ?

Dark, dark upon the restless air,
Streamed out the black flight of her hair ;
Her looks were wild, her garments torn,
Her quivering limbs were waste and worn :
It is—alas ! ye need not tell ;
He knew Sirena's form too well.

He bade her speak, he bade her stand,
And gently raised her by the hand.
' Away !' she cried ; ' thou canst not know
The utter darkness of my woe:

For thou hast learnt—O joy! O bliss !—
What a requited passion is;
But I have only known the pain
Of loving, unbeloved again.'

' Alas,' replied he, ' I have known
A sorrow bitter as thine own,
And though our common tears may flow
From sources separate of woe,
Yet tears can sympathize with tears,
And bleeding hearts have heeding ears.'

She answered not, but, to the ground,
    Dropped down her wild and wond'rous eye ;
Then lifted it and glanced around,
    As if to see if aught were nigh,
And with a voice that seemed to start
In words unbidden from her heart :

''Tis this,' she cried : ' I love thee more
Than ever mortal loved before ;
For this I've sought, for this I've sighed—
To gain your love, to be your bride;
This all-consuming flame within
    Has ate my life into the core ;
I've loved till love became a sin ;
    I've loved till I could love no more.
And now I come to link my soul,
My heart, my life, my love, my whole,
In promise to your destiny,
Or else, O ! listen, Heaven ! I die;
Yon river o'er my corse shall roll,
And heaven or hell receive my soul.'

Amazed he sees, amazed he hears
Her vows, her sighs, her prayers, her tears :
' Alas !' he cried, ' 'tis a fruitless quest
To seek for love in a widowed breast ;
   Go ask the block of shivered ore
For the wealth that is torn from its riven veins ;
   In the beaten straw of the threshing-floor,
Go search and search for the sunburnt grains ;
But away, away, 'tis a fruitless quest
To seek for love in a widowed breast.
To Hermione my love was given,
And it has gone with her to heaven,
And aught that's earthly seeks in vain,
That seeks to win it back again.'

' Yes, yes, it would indeed be vain
To look for gathered fruit again ;
But, bid me hope, that, like the dew
   That lifts the violet's azure eyne,
Love's soothing service may renew
   The hopes, the joys, that once were thine ;
Then, with the birth of other years,
   Renewed affections will arise ;
It is a niggard plant that bears
   One flower alone, then droops and dies.'

' It cannot be ; not love alone—
   For love, indeed, is but the flower
That blooms again, though ten times blown,
   Ay, blows and blooms in one short hour—
But all I am and all I own
Was rooted in my Hermione ;

And now, with bleeding roots, uptorn,
  Withered and dead, how can it be
My heart should bear as it has borne?
  O! love henceforth must be to me
A thing unfelt, a thing unknown,
Save for the soul of Hermione.'

'O! that thy heart should be so kind,
  And yet so cold, and yet so cold;
O! that my love should be so blind,
  And yet so bold, and yet so bold.
Thus is my frantic love returned?
  Thus all I've borne and been repaid?
My prayers denied, my passion spurned,
  My hope, my heart, my all betrayed!
O heartless man, O hopeless maid,
Recall, recall what thou hast said!'

'In vain,' he cried; 'I cannot love,
  And, to accept your love, would be
False to the heart that's gone above,
  And false, unhappy maid, to thee;
No, even though thou wert divine,
Sirena, thou couldst ne'er be mine.'

Away! the cherished dream is past:
Her heart must own the truth at last;
While yet a shade of hope was there,
She could not, would not, know despair;
But now that latest hope has fled,
And rage and hate usurp its stead.

Her flashing eye, her heaving breast,
The passions of her soul expressed,
As lifting her emaciate hand,
As who'd condemn, or who'd command,
' Behold, then, man of flint,' she cried—
' Behold the murderer of your bride !
'Twas I, 'twas I, who made her feel
A rival's, though a sister's, steel ;
Too late I rue the deed—too late
I learn to scorn thee, and to hate.'

Then, ere she well had ceased to speak,
   She dashed the tangling briar away,
And, with a shrill, unearthly shriek,
   Leapt down the rock-encumbered way,
O ! swifter than a hunted hind,
Leaving young Aval far behind.

On, on she flies, nor sound nor sight
Impedes the madness of her flight ;
Now she is lost among the trees,
Emerges now, and on she flees ;
Now where the pathway dips and turns,
Knee-deep in thick-set bracken ferns ;
Then up the mound—O God ! the mound
Of rock 'neath which the river wound !
She's gains the summit ! and she stands
And wildly waves her bleeding hands ;
She looks beneath ! O save her, Heaven,
In vain ! a splash—the stream is riven—
A gush—a groan, 'tis o'er, 'tis o'er,
The stream rolls onward as before.

    *   *   *   *   *

CONCLUSION.

He reached the fatal spot at last,
And, standing helpless and aghast,
Beheld the corse float past ;
And then the white moon slipped into
    The fleece-lined pocket of a cloud,
And wrapped the object from his view,
    As in a shroud.

*   *   *   *

And wrapped the object from his view,
As in a shroud.

CYGNA.

Once more, once more, after so many days
Of hope deferred, of heartache and despair,
I've looked upon the beauty of thy face ;
I've heard thy voice, full of its own strange charm,
Tremble into an ecstasy of song,
Then, like an odour in the breeze, expire.

* * * * *

'Twas in a ruined city by the sea ;
The sun had sunken, and the wave was stained
Red as the lees of wine about the west,
As though a hand had thrown into the sea
A brimming goblet, and the stain remained
To mark where it had fallen.   An ancient wood
Sloped from the misty gorges of the hills,
And stept into the sea ; so that the foam
Sucked at the cold wet sedges of the brim,
And made a sound like kisses in a tomb.
The scene grows fresh before me as I write :
Upon the hull of an abandoned ship
Brooded a cormorant ; the evening wind
Swept like the trail of robes across the sea,

Or, like a soul embodied in a sigh,
Talked to the pine fronds, and the world was still.

How long I'd lingered there I cannot tell,
When, from the darkening forest depths, there stole
A murmur, lute-like, as the western wind
Lost in the chords of a sea-siren's harp
In some lone cavern on the shores of Crete ;
It rose a twilight mist of softest song,
A gossamer of music trembling
Like star-beams in the dimples of the sea ;
Now the wind caught the slender web of sound,
And tossed it lightly as a wood-nymph's veil
Far up among the hills ; and then it burst,
Like a long-stifled sob, adown the vale,
And all the notes ran trembling into one
In long, long trills of sweetness, linked and fused
Like melted pearls upon a thread of flame.

I stood like one who on a summer eve,
Skirting the twilight forests of romance,
Hears the weird revels of the elves and fays ;
Till conquering this instant sense of awe,
Led by the sound, I hurried from the shore,
And following a path beneath the pines,
Plunged deep into the forest central gloom.
Here twilight suddenly was changed to night ;
The long low murmur of the sea grew still,
Only that elfin harmony remained.

And now the path grew steep in its descent ;
The forest growth became less dense, and soon
I saw the violet night above the trees,
And stood upon the purlieus of the wood.

It was a cheerless scene : a dreary marsh
As ever night-hag haunted, or the brain,
Lost in a poppy-sodden dream, conceived.
The stagnant waters, lurid with decay,
Held in their vacant depths the inverted shade
Of the long sedge ; and the rank mere exhaled
A blue dead film, that hung, with bat-like wings,
Brooding above it like a pestilence.
The silence of a mountain tarn was there,
Save when a lost wind sobbed among the reeds,
Alas for Syrinx ! or some startled crane
Rose from its dreams among the moon-cold pools,
And fled with heavy wings into the night.

Upon the margin of the fen there rose
A little ruined chapel ; one pale lamp
Burned through the broken lattice, and its beams,
Upon the heavy waters of the mere,
Lay like a golden creese.   Thence came the sound
That had allured my footsteps from the shore ;
And now more near the ardent music rose,
Clamouring, as with clasped hands and choking voice,
For something lost, lost, lost, for ever lost !
Then, weary with its vain appeal to heaven,
Baffled, undone, despairing, it was still ;
And the low night-wind sobbing in the reeds,
Or the frogs croaking to the vacant moon,
Alone were heard.   Now, when the song had ceased,
I drew more near.   A young and mottled fawn,
Lured from the midnight hollows of the wood,
Lifted its head and fled as I approached.
I gazed upon the ruined sanctuary :
Dim cloistered in a funeral gloom of pines,
An air of desolation and decay

Seemed brooding o'er the place.   The fen's rank ooze
Had gathered into pools among the tombs,
And gleamed among the hollow water-flags
Beneath the cold green walls.   With beating heart
I passed beneath the ruined portico,
And stood within the shrine.

Here all the mystery was revealed to me :
Far down the shadowy chancel, in the light
Scooped out by one pale taper, I beheld
A young and fragile girl ; with head declined,
Seated before an organ, the dim light
Fell round her like a glory, and the wind
Breathed through the broken lattice on her hair,
And stirred the snowy draperies of her robe
Into a tumult.

I might have deemed it some fair spirit form,
Or the girl-god of this forsaken shrine ;
But as I gazed upon her, a great sob
Broke from her bosom, and I knew too well
Such sorrow must be human.   Soon she rose,
And smote again the trembling organ keys,
Until they wailed in concert with the woe
That overflowed her heart, and a great grief
Went out in sobs and song into the night :

' *Though years have passed since last I dwelt*
Upon the music of thy voice,
It still has power to soothe and melt,
And still I hope and still I rejoice.

' A jealous thought, a hasty word,
  And love had fled, and life was changed ;
Too late we learnt how deep we'd erred,
  How mean the cause that had estranged.

' Come back, come back, the past is dead—
  Our love survives, our hearts are free ;
Come, ere the bloom of life has fled,
  Come back, come back, to love and me !'

I heard as in a dream : O life ! O death !
My brain was in a tumult.   Could it be——
I reeled —I caught the mouldering colonnade.
Whence came that sound ?   Was it a dream—a trance?
Could Fancy cheat so cruelly and so well ?
Ah, no, no, no ! I heard, I felt, I knew
It was thy voice, O Cygna ; and the song
That thou didst sing, was one that I had made
When, in the heyday of our love, I sought
A sort of respite from a joy too full,
In singing an imaginary woe—
Alas ! the shadow and the prophecy
Of an impending fate.   Then in a trance,
Scarce conscious of my own identity,
Believing all things, and yet doubting all,
I staggered down the long black aisle to where
The maiden sate ; but ere I reached the spot,
She caught the sound, she started to her feet,
Turned to the darkness, and confronted me ;
Then in the mouldering chancel, 'neath the light
Of one decaying taper, our eyes met,
And, for one wild sweet moment, I beheld
The beauty that had maddened me like wine,

And made my life one long delirium
Of love and hope, of madness and despair ;
Then, with a shriek, she turned from me and fled,
And the pale taper fluttered and went out.

In trembling haste, I reached the small black door
Where the white-robèd form had disappeared,
And, standing there, looked out upon the mere :
No sound of life was there; th' unconscious moon
Gazed at her image tangled in the reeds,
Deep in the silver pools, and the wind moaned,
Alas ! alas! for Syrinx.   That was all.
With sinking heart, I rushed into the night :
'Cygna !' I shouted, and the wind replied.
' Ho ! Cygna, Cygna, Cygna !' I implored,
Until the forest echoed with the name,
Repeating it a thousand times to one.
Hither and thither o'er the wild wide marsh,
Knee-deep among the thronging water-flags,
And splashing in the cold and treacherous pools,
Hour after hour I sought, but sought in vain :
And ever to the night I shouted ' Cygna !'
And ever the wind moaned and the wood mocked.

Then, when the moon had set, I sought again
The desolated shrine : 'twas dark and still ;
My pulses were on fire, my senses reeled,
And fiery figures danced before my eyes
In mad fantastic revels—dark and still ;
With dry hot eyes I gazed upon the mere ;
Ah ! 'twas a dreary spot, dark, silent, cold,
The breeding-place of things that love decay—
Creatures of aspect monstrous and impure :

The spawn of death, the sucklings of disease,
Egyptian, Stygian, vampire-like, unclean.
A dreary spot; a dead sea of despair;
'Twas one of Nature's nightmares—rather say
The fixèd horror of a dead man's dream,
When the wet worm feeds deep upon his brain
And he awakes not ever.

      *   .   *   *   *   *

I sank upon my face on the cold steps,
And knew no more.

FACES.

FACES, faces, faces, faces,
Crowding city streets and places,
Bright with hope and love and laughter, dark with
passion and despair !
O ! the story of the faces :
Angel faces, demon faces,
Faces, faces, faces, faces, faces, faces everywhere.

O ! the beauty of the faces,
Sunny looks and faery graces,
Little wandering gleams of heaven, lost among the ways
of men.
O ! the brightness of the faces,
Maiden faces, children faces,
Beauty in all forms and phases, sojourner and denizen.

O ! the pathos of the faces,
Blighted hopes and dark disgraces,
When the angel robe is spotted and the white soul
stained with sin.
O ! the sorrow of the faces,
Woman faces, youthful faces,
All the harp chords strained and broken ere the anthem
could begin.

O ! the pallor of the faces,
Flying from the cold death places,
Seeking in the shouting highways respite from the hell
within.
O ! the sadness of the faces,
Mother faces, widow faces,
Haggard with the toil and watching by the night-lamp
pale and thin.

O ! the horror of the faces,
Scowling frowns and dark menaces,
Sodden with a thousand vices, hideous with the brand of
Cain.
O ! the terror of the faces,
Felon faces, traitor faces,
Plague-spots on the fair creation, nightmares of a fevered
brain.

Faces, faces, faces, faces,
Crowding city streets and places—
Faces smooth with youth and beauty, faces lined with
age and care.
O ! the story of the faces,
Million, million, million faces,
Faces, faces, faces, faces, faces, faces everywhere.

PAS SEUL.

A FAIRY form,
A fairy face,
A whirl, a storm of silk and lace,
A purple cloud of silk and lace,
An ecstasy of silk and lace,
And the passion deepens apace, apace,
The hot blood purples in brow and face,
We have no thought of time or place,
Our soul is lost in the silk and lace.

O ! a slender foot, a rose-white limb,
Is hidden in the silk and lace—
A rose-white limb, a rose-white limb,
Involved in folds of silk and lace ;
And the fairy figure seems to swim
In purple seas of silk and lace,
To music of the seraphim,
And drunken whorls of silk and lace ;
And a coil of golden, golden hair
Slips down among the silk and lace ;
Her eyes are closed, her bosom bare,
She has no thought of time or place ;
A whirl, a swing, a storm, a fling,
Her soul is in the silk and lace.

A rose-white limb, a rose-white limb,
  O rapture of the silk and lace ;
The golden hair, the bosom bare,
  On, on wild song of silk and lace !
O golden hair, O golden hair,
O angel bosom white and bare,
  O song, O song of silk and lace !
  And over all, a pale rapt face
Gleams out above the silk and lace :
A muse, an elf, a girl, a grace,
O story of the pale rapt face,
O passion of the silk and lace,
A muse, an elf, a girl, a grace,
Cease, cease wild song of silk and lace !
O sorrow of the pale rapt face,
O madness of the silk and lace !
Who does not love the pale rapt face ?
Cease, cease, O song of silk and lace.

RECORDED IMPRESSIONS.

A RHAPSODY ON MUSIC.

I.

As one who, in the pride of manhood, frets
　Beneath a power he dare not disobey;
Who brooks the bond that trammels and besets,
　And hides the strength 'twere madness to display;
So, conscious of its strength, yet fain to own
　The dominating influence of man,
Reserving half the thunder of its tone,
　The song of songs began.

Then, strong as God, it rose,
　And shouting to the echoes that stood hushed,
　Waiting the signal of arising, rushed
Swift as a mountain-wolf upon its foes.

II.

Hark ! hark ! hark !
Pattering, babbling, tripping, trilling ;
Deepening, hurrying, panting, thrilling ;
Fling and flight, and rush and rout ;
　Wild attack and passioned pause ;
Dash and dare, and shock and shout ;
　Careless clamour and mad applause.

A clangour of golden doors, a jasper fret and a diamond
    jar,
Tremblant as a river reed, palpitant as the evening
    star,
The charge and the crash of the warring spheres, the
    heaven-quake of the thunder car ;
Pausing now as if enamoured of the beauty it creates,
Then the passion shouts and thunders, baffling at the
    clangèd gates,
Clamouring for the peace of heaven, and the mercy of
    the fates.

    Then the music droops and falls,
      Lapsing down liquid alleys of soft song,
      And dying like a spirit voice among
    The phantom-haunted shadows of old walls.

III.

Again the passion quickens, swift and sweet,
A cowslip-muffled rush of fairy feet ;
      O sweet, sweet, sweet—
      A hurried ecstasy, a panting bliss,
      A kiss, kiss, kiss, kiss, kiss,
With hot face buried in the throbbing cleft
Of a white bosom, in a mænad theft
Of all consuming kisses ;
A breathless incoherence of soft sound ;
    A bee drone in the passion flowers ;
An odour cloud of music ; a deep swound
    Among the poppies in the fierce noon hours ;
    A wild sob-lullaby, in showers
Of hot mouth-kisses drowned.

IV.

And then it changes to a mad despair,
   A passion of farewells,
   An agony in the trampled asphodels,
A sobbing, sobbing on the golden hair
   Of a dead child ;
The wailing of the winds and waves,
   On alien shores oblique and wild,
Among the cold sea-caves ;
   A fluting in the panic reeds,
A wizard rune,
Wild and shrill, and out of tune,
   'Mid hecatombs of poison weeds,
From cold night altars to the moon.

V.

A child, in pillow clefts, at night
   I pressed my eyes, and seemed to see
Fantastic whorls of coloured light,
And trembling forms obscurely bright,
Flicker and dance before my sight,
   With freaks of maddest phantomry.

And now such pictures, interwove
   With subtlest trace of bygone thought,
Before the spirit vision move
   And fade before their light is caught :
Brief glimpses of moon-haunted coves,
And orchard glades, and twilight groves,
   And sunny cattle closes ;
A cottage in among the hills,

With wall-flowers in the window-sills,
  And lattices half blind with roses ;
A half-seen wing, a broken halo-crown,
  And lips stretched out and pouting to be kissed ;
Fair starry eyes, and togas slipping down
  O'er arms more soft and white than fancy wist ;
Swift glimpse of ocean hall and siren grot,
And harps, and flowers, and forests, and what not.

VI.

Then mournful as a bittern's cry,
  With black wings to the setting sun,
The music seemed to sink and die,
  And soon the song of songs was done.

CONSTANT.

Though other hearts may chance to claim
    The homage of an idle sigh,
Yet is my love a constant flame,
    A vestal fire that cannot die.

These are the lights that come and go,
    Thou art the fixed star of my fate,
To beckon o'er the polar snow,
    And point to where the angels wait.

The winds that on a summer eve
    Trail their light skirts across the mere,
Stir not the depths, and, passing, leave
    A moment's trace and disappear.

BUT O! BUT O!

AHA ! the fair, the more than fair,
　She slept beneath the mooted hay ;
He stole upon her unaware,
　He brushed the crumpled curls away,
　　　And then—
　　　But O ! but O !

Aha ! that brow so summer-tann'd,
　Aha ! those lips so soft and sweet ;
He seized upon her sunburnt hand,
　She woke, she started to her feet,
　　　And then—
　　　But O ! but O !

Aha ! the moon so cold and pale ;
　Aha ! the lonely linden-tree ;
And still he breathed the same old tale,
　And still she blushed if he could see ;
　　　And then—
　　　But O ! but O !

Aha ! the day, the flowers, the bells ;
　The lingering hours, the fading west ;
The home among the hills and dells ;
　The hints, the smiles, and all the rest,
　　　And then—
　　　But O ! but O !

HINTS: A PASTORAL.

O, THROUGH the cornfields day by day,
  And morn and night, and night and morn,
He chanced to go the self-same way,
  And passed her in among the corn ;
    And so may you, sir.

   *   *   *   *   *

O, all the pinks were over-blown
  That bloomed above the village well ;
He met her there—alone, alone—
  And doffed his hat and wished her well ;
    And so may you, sir.

   *   *   *   *   *

O, hard and high the meadow stile,
  The sun had set an hour or more ;
With half a blush and half a smile,
  He held his hand to help her o'er ;
    And so may you, sir.

   *   *   *   *   *

O, dark and deep the beechen boughs
  That stretched above the waterfall ;
He breathed the first of loving vows,
  He swore to be her all in all ;
    And so may you, sir.

   *   *   *   *   *

O, brightly flashed the morning dew,
    The bridal bells rang far and wide ;
He swore he would be loyal and true,
    He clasped and claimed his queen and bride ;
And so may you, sir, and so adieu, sir.

———————

KATE: A PASTORAL.

AND the bells, the bells, the tumbling bells
    Shall reel and peal through the livelong day;
And they'll deck the church with blooming birch,
    And the cherry bloom and the may, the may;
'So kiss me, Kate, and we'll be married o' Sunday.'

And you shall have rings and golden things,
    And satin shoes as white as milk,
And coloured bows and high clock hose,
    And a glittering gown of silk, of silk;
'So kiss me, Kate, and we'll be married o' Sunday.'

And servants shall wait on my Lady Kate,
    Like a maiden queen of a high degree;
And garlands rare shall bind your hair,
    Dragged from the mouth of the bee, the bee;
'So kiss me, Kate, and we'll be married o' Sunday.'

And the true and the tried of the country-side
    Shall haste to bless the happy pair;
And all shall vow that never till now
    Was a bride, was a bride, so fair, so fair;
'So kiss me, Kate, and we'll be married o' Sunday.'

THE BALLAD OF THE LADY OF THE RHINE.

I.

Bright, bright was the day of our love, Lady,
But dark, dark, dark, was the morrow ;
Bright as a poet's happiness,
Dark as a poet's sorrow.

II.

Deep in the sunny south, Lady,
Deep in the land of the vine,
Where your lattice pushed its roses back
On the sleep of the moonlit Rhine.

III.

And we loved with a love that was madness, Lady,
And we vowed with a vow that was sin ;
We had no care how the day might end—
No thought how the night might begin.

IV.

But your kinsmen proud and cold, Lady,
Bore you off to an unknown clime ;
Ah ! you were dowered with a lordly name,
And I—with the gift of rhyme.

v.

Brief, brief was the day of our love, Lady,
  But long, long, long, was the morrow ;
Brief as a poet's happiness,
  Long as a poet's sorrow.

THE PIER: A NOCTURNE.

THE old stone pier across the harbour's mouth ;
The odour of the sea and of the ships.

'Twas evening on the waters ; one by one
The red-sailed boats came in across the bar,
And, like a troop of phantoms, slowly passed
Into their haven underneath the hills,
And silence settled down upon the sea.

There ran a lurid seam across the west,
Where closed the edges of night's secret veil,
Before the sun's high altar place ;
The moon's thin aftermath of lucent light
Waved in the fields of air ; and one by one
The silver-petalled stars throbbed into bloom,
Trembling in the intensity of heaven.
A berg of cloud, whose ragged fringe had caught
A nimbus from the moon, was floating down
A violet tract of sky ;
The harbour lights flung crooked spears of gold
Into the shivering waters of the bay ;
And where the dim port lantern gleamed, there fell
Libations of red light into the sea.

There lay the black hulls of the ported sloops,
Couchant and straining at the cable-chains

Like sea-hounds on the leash ; the ship-lights gleamed
Like stars in the dark firmament of sea ;
The mendicant wind moaned out a hollow tale ;
And the cold waves were babbling to themselves,
Or, in the caverns of the black-toothed coast,
Scheming the winter storms.

The valley town smoked in among its hills,
And to the clouds breathed up a mist of light,
Dantean exhalation, such as hung
Lurid above the flaming pits of sin.
The storm of life was beating in its streets :
I felt its lurid breath upon my cheek,
As down the smoking gorges of the hills
It trembled like a heated furnace blast,
And died upon the sea.
                              Beautiful night !
Let the worn moral of thy mystery lie
Unpointed here ; there is a sense that feels,
Without th' unprofitable toil of verse,
The teachings of thy beauty ; let the stars,
The mystery of the night and of the sea,
Whisper their own sweet tale into thy heart :
For beauty is the essence of all good ;
So he who loves is purified, and he
Who teaches beauty teaches holiness.

THE END.

Elliot Stock, Paternoster Row, London.

www.ingramcontent.com/pod-product-compliance
Lightning Source LLC
Chambersburg PA
CBHW020806020726
47495CB00008B/2614